Boy Minus Girl

Boy Minus Girl

RICHARD UHLIG

Alfred A. Knopf
NEW YORK

THIS IS A BORZOI BOOK PUBLISHED BY ALFRED A. KNOPF

VISIT US ON THE WEB! WWW.RANDOMHOUSE.COM/TEENS

EDUCATORS AND LIBRARIANS, FOR A VARIETY OF TEACHING TOOLS, VISIT US AT
WWW.RANDOMHOUSE.COM/TEACHERS

LIBRARY OF CONGRESS CATALOGING-IN-PUBLICATION DATA
UHLIG, RICHARD ALLEN.
BOY MINUS GIRL / RICHARD UHLIG. — 1ST ED.
P. CM.
SUMMARY: WHEN HIS CHARMING BUT IRRESPONSIBLE UNCLE COMES TO VISIT HIS SMALL KANSAS HOMETOWN, FOURTEEN-YEAR-OLD LES ECKHARDT HOPES TO GET TIPS FROM HIM ABOUT SUCCEEDING WITH GIRLS, BUT HE LEARNS MUCH MORE IMPORTANT LESSONS FROM HIS STODGY AND PREDICTABLE PARENTS AND FRIENDSHIPS WITH A LESBIAN CLASSMATE AND ONE OF UNCLE RAY'S FORMER GIRLFRIENDS.
ISBN 978-0-375-83968-9 (TRADE) — ISBN 978-0-375-93968-6 (LIB. BDG.)
[1. INTERPERSONAL RELATIONS—FICTION. 2. UNCLES—FICTION. 3. RESPONSIBILITY—FICTION. 4. LESBIANS—FICTION. 5. SEX—FICTION. 6. KANSAS—HISTORY—20TH CENTURY—FICTION.] I. TITLE.
PZ7.U32578Bo 2008
[FIC]—DC22
2008002566

THE TEXT OF THIS BOOK IS SET IN 11.5-POINT NOFRET.

PRINTED IN THE UNITED STATES OF AMERICA
DECEMBER 2008
10 9 8 7 6 5 4 3 2 1
FIRST EDITION

To my mother
—R.U.

PART ONE

Seduction Tip Number 1:

Tongue Twister

The Seductive Man knows his tongue is an invaluable erotic instrument, which must be exercised daily. Stick it out as far as it will go, then pull it back deep into your mouth. Do this ten times rapidly. Next, flutter your tongue like the wings of a hummingbird for three minutes. Soon you'll be ready to pleasure her with the Velvet Buzz Saw.

Mom, Dad, and I sit at the oval kitchen table, trying to eat Mom's meat loaf. In the window above the sink, the yellow lace curtains frolic in the hot May wind, diluting the strange scent wafting off the meat. To my right, Mom, in her starched nurse's uniform and red-checkered apron, primly sips her iced tea. To my left, Dad, in his dress shirt and tie, squints at the *Wichita Eagle-Beacon* lying beside his plate.

"Uh, Dad," I say, "the talent show is a week from Friday."

"Uh-huh," he says to the newspaper.

"And, well, my magical vanishing box is nowhere near done."

"Not tonight, son, I'm bushed."

Beneath the table I'm fondling a red grape, massaging the soft skin with my fingertips. This is an exercise recommended in *The Seductive Man* by M.—a book my best friend, Howard, is loaning me—to condition my hands for a woman's nipples. Someday soon I will be performing this task expertly on Charity Conners, my dream girl.

Dad points to the newspaper but looks at Mom. "Says here this could be the worst tornado season in decades."

"Mmm," Mom says absently. (We are quite used to this sort of announcement from Dad.)

"After dinner I'll go down and make sure the shelter is stocked with enough provisions to last us a couple weeks," Dad says. "In case the house is blown away," he adds.

Dad fears for us all, all of the time—natural disasters, nuclear war, rabid skunks, Lyme disease–carrying ticks, mosquitoes whose bites will make our brains swell up and burst. To Dad the whole world is a virtual land mine of deadly diseases and impending disasters.

I pipe up with: "Maybe this would be a good time for us to go on a trip. Get out of the vicinity of the twisters. Y'know, in three weeks my summer vacation starts. What if we all went to Florida?"

"Florida?" Dad looks at me as if I had just suggested we pitch a tent on Mount Saint Helens.

"The Schneiders are driving to Epcot Center for their summer vacation," I offer.

"You don't say," Mom says. "The Schneiders still owe your father a hundred dollars for setting Tommy's broken arm last January. But I guess for some people a luxurious vacation is more important than paying their debts."

Dad shakes his head. "I can't leave town. I've got a hospital full of patients. Besides, Florida is boiling hot in the summer and your mother's prone to heatstroke."

"Speaking of hot, when can we turn on the air-conditioning?" I ask Mom, unbuttoning my shirt a notch to drive home the point.

"We can easily get by with fans for at least another month," Mom, the family accountant, announces. "I refuse to pay for any more electricity than I absolutely have to. The electricity rates this town charges, why, it's highway robbery!"

"But, Mom, I've heard your very own personal physician say that you're prone to heatstroke," I remind her.

"You know, Les," Mom continues, "you make it

sound as if air–conditioning is your birthright. You kids today don't appreciate how spoiled you are with all your luxurious conveniences."

Luxuries? We are practically the *only* people in town without a dishwasher or cable TV or a garbage disposal. Dad won't allow a microwave in the house for fear of radiation leakage, and the only reason we have a new TV is because Mom won it at a raffle at the IGA. She drives a ten–year–old Buick she inherited from her great–aunt Irma, and we live in the same humble house Dad grew up in. And we aren't poor: Dad has a very busy medical practice, and Mom works, too.

As I stare at the meat loaf and massage the grape, I try to imagine Dad fondling Mom. How could they ever get past the rising cost of groceries and the constant threat of salmonella enough to get in the mood? Yet, here I am. How? Was I adopted? If I was, who are my real parents? Do they ever eat in restaurants? Do they like to travel and socialize and go shopping? Maybe they live in a high–rise in New York City, like the Jeffersons, and stay up late with their glamorous friends, trading witticisms over martinis and discussing the latest Broadway shows. I look at my mother and see we have the exact same light–blue eye color; I look at Dad and see my big brow.

God, I have nothing to look forward to this summer. God, I'm in a slump. God, I need something. Something more. Big–time.

Brring-ring.

"Got it!" I grab the wall-mounted phone by the fridge. "Eckhardt residence."

"Who's this?" a deep, male smoker's voice asks, from what sounds like a pay phone on the side of a busy highway.

"It's Les."

"Lester the Mo-lester! Hell, this is your uncle Ray! Remember me?!"

Remember him? The last time I saw him, he was passed out, facedown drunk, on our lawn!

"Hi, Uncle Ray!"

Dad smiles while Mom puts her hand to her mouth. My uncle Ray is Dad's only sibling. He was here last for Grandpa Eckhardt's funeral, at which he sported a black leather jacket, torn blue jeans, and no tie. His girlfriend wore purple eye shadow and a low-cut dress that barely contained her gigantic bazookas. I was in the fifth grade and had never seen anyone drunk before (or since).

"Your old man around?!" he shouts over a passing truck horn.

"Uh, sure, Uncle Ray, one sec." I hand the phone to Dad.

"How the hell are you, little brother?!"

I see Mom wince at Dad's coarse language.

"Uh-huh...right..." Dad nods and smiles, wrapping the phone cord around his index finger. "Well, that would be just fine, Ray. Look forward to it. We'll leave the light on for ya, as they say."

Uncle Ray is coming! Will he bring his generously endowed girlfriend with him? *Please please please please please.*

Dad hands me the phone and I hang it up.

"Ray's already on his way here," Dad announces. "Says he'd like to stay with us for a while."

"Is he ... coming alone?" I ask hopefully.

Dad nods and takes a bite of meat loaf.

"What does he want?" Mom asks.

Wiping the corner of his mouth with the cloth napkin, Dad says, "Just to visit. We are his only family after all."

"I wish you had asked me before you told him yes," Mom says. "We just don't have the space since we got rid of the bed in the spare room."

"He can sleep on my bottom bunk," I volunteer.

"That settles it, then," Dad says.

Is this the drama I have been aching for? Perhaps Uncle Ray had ESP and picked up on my plea? Or maybe Jesus decided to throw me a bone for not jerking off for the past two days. Uncle Ray is by far my favorite relative. Over the years I have absorbed little snippets of conversation between my parents concerning him: he was a lady's man, a professional guitarist; he drank way too much, had lived all over and done all sorts of un-Christian things. My cool uncle Ray. I pop the grape in my mouth and chew on the possibilities.

"I'm telling you," Howard says to me over the phone, "Lurch *is* Thing."

"He is *so* not," I say as I dry the last of the dinner plates.

"First, have you ever seen Lurch and Thing in the same room together? Don't think so. Secondly, look at the thumbs. Lurch and Thing have the same thumbs!"

"But the end credit for Thing is 'Itself,'" I say. "Not 'Lurch.'"

"Duh! Of course they're not going to say 'Lurch.' That would take away the mystique of Thing."

"I don't know, How. I'm thinking I have seen 'em in the same room together."

"Well, I haven't and I've seen *every* episode," he concludes. "What're you doing? Wanna come over and play Space Invaders?"

"Can't," I say, and close the cupboard. "I have to clean my room for my uncle."

"Lame-o." Click, dial tone.

I tie off the kitchen garbage bag and lug it out to the garage, dropping it beside the wooden frame of what is supposed to be my Chinese vanishing box. About five months ago, when I signed up to do a magic act for eighth-grade talent night, Dad promised me he'd build the phone-booth-sized plywood contraption. It's supposed to be the highlight of my act.

Up in my slope-ceilinged, top-floor bedroom, I put fresh sheets on the bottom bunk for Uncle Ray while singing along to "We Are the World" on the radio. I usually don't like adults in my space, but Uncle Ray isn't a normal grown-up.

The state news comes on the radio: late last night a nightclub owner in Kansas City was shot dead in his club, and fifty grand is missing from the wall safe.

"The assailant, believed to be a tall, dark-haired Caucasian male in his late thirties, is considered armed and dangerous," the sonorous baritone voice announces. "Authorities are urging people to be on the lookout for..."

I clear everything off the top of my dresser except for the second-place trophy I won at the Tri-County 4-H Fair talent show last year. I'm hoping Uncle Ray will ask me what I won for, and then I'll proceed to dazzle him with my magic tricks. After dusting off my framed autographed picture of David Copperfield, my idol, which hangs on the green wall beside the window, I empty my top two dresser drawers for Uncle Ray's things and relocate my secret stash of nudie pictures to the back of my closet. My collection is mostly bra models from Mom's nursing-uniform catalogs and the topless African women from Dad's *National Geographics*.

I spray the room with Mountain Mist air freshener,

then settle on my beanbag and open my biology book. Tucked deep inside is *The Seductive Man*. I pick up where I left off before dinner. Page 62: "Think of your tongue as an electric eel causing a slight shock sensation wherever it touches her. Run it over her earlobes, neck, mouth, nose, and eyes. Dwell on her nipples and breasts, swirling and sucking as you go. . . ."

Close my eyes, try to imagine myself doing this to Charity Conners. *Oh, Charity. Oh God. Oh—*I run to the bathroom, lock the door, reach under the sink behind the towels, remove my special, empty Skin So Soft bottle. Yeah, fits just right. Afterward, lying on the floor, I am disgusted with myself.

Dear Jesus . . . please forgive me. If I don't jerk off for a whole week, would You please make me brave enough to talk to Charity? I humbly beseech You in Your Name. Amen.

After my shower I stare at my naked body in the bathroom mirror and flex my arm muscles. *Must gain weight. I'm built like a Popsicle stick. Maybe I should start doing push-ups to bulk up.* I turn and glance at my side and back. *Man, am I white. Like Elmer's glue. Gotta get a tan this summer. Who would want to fool around with an albino? Now my profile—ugh! My honker is humongous. I look like a toucan. Next, my smile—the braces—year and a half before they come off. And last but hopefully not least, my pecker. Normal? Too small? It looks like a Little Smoky with two acorns. In the shower in gym class, I think I look smaller than some of the other guys. But how about when I have a boner? My boner feels huge. Will Charity Conners ever find my Little Smoky and acorns sexy?*

While doing push-ups in my room, I hear my parents' muffled voices reverberating through the floor vent (their bedroom is right below mine). I lie down and press my ear to the grate.

"You know Ray only comes here when he wants something," Mom insists.

"If my brother wants to visit us, he'll always be welcome." Dad sounds very tired. "It's been almost four years, Bev."

"Well, he better not ask you for money again. And I don't like that he's staying in Les's room. Heaven knows what diseases he'll bring with him, the way he lives."

Brring-ring. Dad answers: "Hello. Uh-huh . . . Get an EKG and vitals. I'll be right over." I hear Dad leave for the hospital.

I switch on my little clamp light and try to learn more about the female G-spot, but I can't concentrate. Mom has a point: it is weird that Uncle Ray is suddenly coming to visit after all these years. And then it hits me: could Uncle Ray be the assailant the authorities are looking for? The description the radio announcer gave certainly fits. Is he coming here to hide out? *You're crazy,* I assure myself. *Uncle Ray is a lover, not a killer.* Still . . .

There's a knock on my door, and Mom appears in her floor-length, cat-print cotton nightgown, her hair wrapped in pink curlers. "Les, it's almost time for Johnny Carson."

***

Mom and I are seated on the living-room sofa stuffing popcorn into our mouths and cracking up over Billy Crystal's "Dahling, you rook mahvelous" routine. For all of Mom's disdain for obscenities, she loves to laugh and stay up late to watch *The Tonight Show*. It's been our ritual for years. During the commercials I turn down the volume, stand in front of the TV, put on Grandpa's old cowboy hat, and do my best President Reagan impersonation: "Well, Nancy, the evil empire is trying to destroy the very fabric of our great nation."

I remove the cowboy hat and switch to the shaky voice of Katharine Hepburn: "No, Ronnie, it's me, Katie. Nancy sent me to tell you she's leaving you for Gorbachev. She finds his birthmahk irresistible."

Now I'm Reagan: "Well, in that case I think I'll take a nap."

Mom laughs so hard she snorts a little—nothing makes me happier than when I make Mom crack up.

After *The Tonight Show*, once Mom goes to bed, I try to stay up for Uncle Ray by practicing some new magic tricks in front of my dresser mirror.

Can't stay awake, too sleepy. I scribble a note and place it on the dresser:

Welcome, Uncle Ray! Bottom bunk is all yours—
I even cleaned the sheets! Sorry I wasn't awake
when you got here.
Love, Les

Seduction Tip Number 2:

The Breast Test

Place two large water-filled balloons a few inches apart on a flat, firm surface. As if you're going to perform a push-up, place the palm of each hand flat on either side of the balloons. Keeping your back straight, lower your chest onto the balloons. If you can perform this without exploding the balloons, you're applying the right amount of pressure on her breasts. Start with five, increase daily.

Mom's voice: "Les dear, it's time to get ready for school."

Sunlight pours in through the beige curtains, and it takes me a moment to realize I'm in my sleeping bag on the floor in my parents' bedroom. I slowly remember why: in the middle of the night Dad shook me awake.

"Your mother and I got to worrying," he said. "With this Kansas City killer at large, we'd feel better if you slept in our room tonight."

I remember grunting and turning away from him, but he grasped my shoulder and turned me back. "Remember those Clutters. Can't be too careful."

The Clutters, a Kansas farm family, were robbed and slaughtered in their house one night by some drifters— *almost thirty years ago.* Someone even wrote a book about it. I don't think Dad has had a sound night's sleep ever since.

In the painfully bright morning light Mom hovers over me, smiling, her red apron over her nurse uniform. "Your breakfast is almost ready."

"Did Uncle Ray come?"

Mom's smile drops. "At four-thirty this morning. Tell me, what kind of guest shows up at four-thirty in the morning? Now hop to."

I push open my bedroom door to the scent of tobacco and musky-smelling aftershave, and the sound of deep, male snoring. There's my uncle Ray, all six feet three of him. He's lying on his back, his right arm slung over his eyes, his mouth hanging open, face looking kind of whiskery. A small silver loop hangs from his right earlobe, and his long sideburns are flecked with gray. A manly forest of black hair carpets his bare chest, and on his upper left arm a red dragon tattoo spews flames. On the floor beside the bed stand a pair of stylish, low–sided black boots with big silver buckles.

I walk to the window, go to drop the blinds, and see, parked in front of our house, a kick–ass sky–blue 1960s convertible. The sun reflects off its sleek chrome, and I pray Uncle Ray will take me for a spin in it.

Tiptoe to the closet, reach for my clothes, and spot four classy–looking shirts, all in deep colors, hanging perfectly on wooden hangers. And there on the floor of my closet sits a large black suitcase. What is making it bulge so much? Fifty thousand stolen dollars? I reach down to grab my sneakers and spot a big bottle of brown liquid with a Jack Daniel's label behind his suitcase.

In the kitchen Mom turns the sputtering bacon. Seated at the table, his hair plastered down, in his usual white shirt and tie, Dad stares pensively at the front page of the Wichita paper. "A Pentagon spokesman is quoted as saying: 'A Soviet nuclear missile could strike anywhere in the U.S. with only a fifteen–minute warning.'"

I sit across from him and say, "Isn't Uncle Ray's con- vertible awesome?"

"Convertibles are nothing but foolish," Mom grouses. "When they flip over, there's not a thing to protect you."

Dad drops the newspaper and says to me, "Last night you said you wanted to go on a family vacation this summer. Well, I think I've come up with just the place."

"You have?"

He nods. "Rock City."

"Huh?"

"It's this big field filled with massive rocks—some as big as our house!—formed millions of years ago before the Ice Age. Can you imagine?"

"So . . . it's just . . . a bunch of rocks?" I ask.

"Not *just* a bunch of rocks. Big *geological* rocks. Some shaped like birdbaths and turtles. It's the only place on earth to see such a thing and—get this!—it's right here in Kansas. Only about an hour's drive from here."

"That sounds *terrific*, honey!" Mom says, setting the plate of bacon on the table. "That way we won't even have to pay for a motel room."

"I mean, why go all the way to Florida when Kansas has such a fascinating and educational landmark?" Dad asks. "You can't go wrong if you stick to your own backyard."

We're still in Kansas, Toto. Forever.

Twenty minutes later I'm on my way to school, coasting my Dirt King bike down Tripp Street hill, when I hear a familiar voice coming at me from behind: "Hey, Leth-bian!"

Shit! My heart speeds up and I pedal like a madman.

"What'th your hurry?! Y'got a boyfriend waiting?!"

I pump harder, but Brett the Brute's Sting–Ray bike churns up effortlessly on my left.

"I'm talking to you, faggot!"

I swerve right, cutting through the vacant gravel lot of the Phillips 66 station. When I veer onto Broadway, Brett is right there, greeting me with: "Nith try, cock breath!"

He sticks out his big black sneaker, and the next thing I know, I'm sprawled on my back on the grass of Flood & Son Mortuary. There Brett straddles me, his butt pressing painfully into my abdomen. I try to wriggle free, but the lard ass must weigh 250 pounds. Brett has been held back several times and is twice the size of a normal eighth grader. The terror of Harker City Junior High, Brett once broke my best friend Howard's nose in gym class. He has threatened several of our teachers, and Principal Cheavers is frightened to death of him. Last summer he stole a car and was put in juvie.

Brett's meaty, callused hands press my face sideways into the dewy grass.

"When I thay you pull over, you do it, y'hear me?!" Brett isn't a patron of deodorant or hand–hygiene. "Y'hear me, Dickhardt?!"

Through the grass blades I spot a yellow school bus. Staring out the window at me, gape–mouthed, is Charity Conners.

Brett shoves my head harder into the grass. "Thay you're thorry."

"I'm thorry!"

He eases up. "That'th more like it. Now, I have thomething for ya." His rough lips stretch into a devilish, snaggletoothed grin. He digs his butt into my abdomen and rips the loudest, longest fart in Dickerson County.

When I look up, the school bus and Charity, my Charity, are gone. Alas. And—*crap*!

" 'At' is not a place, people!" declares Mrs. Crockmeister, her narrow-set little eyes glimmering as she holds up a red-inked paper. "Who lives at 'at'? No one! How many times do I have to tell you this?!"

I'm staring three seats ahead and one row to the left—where *she* sits. Her shiny, helmet-like black hair hangs to her ears and contrasts beautifully with her white skin. I very much want to kiss that long, long neck. Among the many obstacles: I haven't said one word to her since the fifth grade, three years ago, when I called her "Turkey Tits."

You see, in elementary school I found Charity Conners totally annoying: she was always the first to finish her schoolwork, made the best grades, and acted real superior to everyone. In Mrs. Olsen's fifth-grade class, we were assigned neighboring desks and pretty much ignored each other. Then, one Friday afternoon during the *Weekly Reader* current-events film-strip, I whispered something to Howard, who sat on the other side of Charity. She turned to me and said, "Hush up, Lester, I'm trying to listen."

"Why don't *you* shut up, Turkey Tits."

She blinked twice, then flipped me the bird. When I came into school the following Monday, Charity's desk was empty and Mrs. Olsen informed us she had moved to St. Louis with her folks. Good riddance, Turkey Tits. Or so I thought.

Then, a month ago, there I was, seated in this very room, when the door opened and Principal Cheavers ushered in the sexy new girl with the cool haircut. My breath was taken at the sight of her swimming-pool-blue eyes and pillowy lips. I was instantly in love. She was so . . . not Harker City.

"Everyone, this is Charity Conners," he said. "You might remember her; she lived here a few years back. Please make her feel welcome."

I couldn't believe it. Where was that annoying girl with long black braids and the clacking retainer?

"Ahoy, mateys, it's my goil, Olive Oyl," Howard whispered over the top of his opened *Guinness Book of World Records* upon seeing her tallish frame step through the doorway.

"I think she looks . . . exotic," I said.

"She has a face like one of my mom's lady-head planters," Howard retorted.

I silently, vehemently disagreed; she was pretty—really pretty—just not in the usual cheerleadery way.

"Still doesn't mean I wouldn't do her," said Howard as he made a little hip-thrusting motion under his desk. With his Bugs Bunny teeth, marshmallowy body, and incessant spouting of trivia, Howard stands even less of a chance of getting laid than I do.

Plus, I think, he overcompensates for the fact his dad is the ultra-uptight Reverend Bachbaugh.

Charity Conners doesn't dress like the other girls, either. No jeans and white canvas sneakers. She wears long black dresses, strings of pearls—and worn bowling shoes! Word has it her dad is an engineer on the railroad and was transferred back to Harker City.

Every time I approach Charity, I feel my face heat up and I scurry like a scaredy-cat in the opposite direction. Talking to cute girls has always made me nervous, but this particular girl—she might very well recall that I'm the guy who once called her Turkey Tits.

Last week I was down at Ratcliff's Pharmacy getting a root-beer float with Howard when I spotted a new men's cologne called Instinct. "Made from the musk of wild boars!" the label declared. "Men, let pheromones do the work for you. Warning: women may violently throw themselves at you."

"Please, please don't tell me you're going to buy that," Howard said.

"Says here it's scientifically proven to make females go wild," I said, uncapping the bottle and sniffing.

Howard cringed. "Smells like Aqua Velva Barnyard. The only thing you're going to attract with that are sows. *Soo-eeee.*"

But I believe in science, and I instantly forked over the ten bucks. The next day I dabbed it behind my ears and on my wrists and made a point of standing behind Charity in the cafeteria line. She sneezed. Twice. The following day I splashed it on my chest, arms, and legs.

"Oink!" Howard ran up to me at my locker and started dry-humping my leg. "I love you! Oink! I must have you! Oink!"

Now, back in English class, I look at Charity, who is reading the biggest magazine I've ever seen, something called *Interview*. Soon, soon, soon, I *will* talk to her!

After third period, at the first-floor water fountain, I glance at the sign-up sheet for the eighth-grade talent show taped to the wall and see a new entry: "Howard Bachbaugh—break dancing." I beeline to Howard's locker, which is chock-full of books containing pointless facts: *Ripley's Believe It or Not! Mind-Boggling Facts, The Book of Lists, This Will Surprise You.*

"What is this about you break-dancing?" I ask.

"That's correct," Howard says, a little snootily. "I've perfected my moonwalk. Among other things."

"Such as?"

"You'll see next Friday night." And he saunters off, kinda cocky-like. Very un-Howard.

I turn to walk away just as Mom, in her nursing uniform and little winged hat, strides past, her white orthopedic shoes squeaking on the red linoleum floor. I spin back to the sign-up sheet, pretending not to see her. Sometimes she comes over to my locker "just to chat" or to bring me something for lunch—once she kissed me in front of everyone! Mom is our school nurse. But there are barely ninety kids in the entire junior high, so she only comes in on Mondays or when there's an emergency. The rest of the week she works at Dad's office.

Please understand that I don't blame my lack of popularity on the fact that my dad has touched the scrotum of nearly every guy in school, or that my mom shows sex-ed films and gives guest lectures about menstruation and nocturnal emissions in health class. No, I know that I am unpopular because I am not a jock. Football, the sport that determines where one stands in the food chain, is simply "too dangerous" according to Mom, and according to me. I hate the idea of wearing all those pads and slamming into someone. At Dad's urging I went out for basketball in the sixth grade. I didn't make a single basket the entire season, never mastered a layup, and resented having to stay after school and miss *The Andy Griffith Show.*

Barney Fife is my hero. Skinny, awkward, eyes

bulging out like a fish. And he *still* manages to have a girlfriend. Thelma Lou, and sometimes "sweet" Juanita.

When I get home that afternoon, Uncle Ray's Corvette still gleams in front of our plain little house. I open my bedroom door, and once my eyes adjust to the dimness, I freeze at the sight of Uncle Ray lying on the bottom bunk, reading *The Seductive Man*. Blood rushes to my face. Has he been snooping through my stuff? Did I leave it out?

I clear my throat. "Hey, Uncle Ray!"

He turns to me. "Lester the Mo–lester!"

Tossing the book aside, he wraps his hand around the rail of the upper bunk, pulls himself up, swinging his legs to the floor, and stands.

"Lookit you!" He bear–hugs me, pulling me off the floor, then sets me down. "You must be the star of the basketball team."

"Not even close."

"Say, thanks for letting me crash in your room."

"No problem."

"And hey, you need privacy to jerky the old turkey, just give me the word and I'll make myself scarce."

It takes me a moment to figure out what he means, and then I try hard not to look shocked. My parents never joke about stuff like that.

"So, tell me, kid, you got a girlfriend?"

"I'm working on it."

He holds up *The Seductive Man*. "Yeah, well, don't you believe any of this new-age, sensitive-guy bullshit. It won't get you halfway to first base." He flips to the back cover and the soft-focus photo of the author: a bald, middle-aged man with a gray beard and black turtle-neck, his sensitive face tilted a little, his caterpillar eye-brows furrowed thoughtfully. All he needs is a pipe to look like Mr. Sanderson, my science teacher—and a permanent bachelor.

"You can't tell me this douche bag is getting any," Uncle Ray says.

I dutifully crack up, mostly to cover my humiliation.

He thumbs through the pages and reads in a lisp-ing voice. "'The first rule to making her love you is to be your kind, interesting, sensitive self. Women want a friend first and foremost.'" He snaps the book closed, causing me to flinch, and flings it onto my desk. "No. They. Don't. Chicks want excitement and fun! Lots of it!"

This is why I *love* Uncle Ray: he's the only grown-up I know who talks to me like I'm a man.

"Is that your secret to getting women, Uncle Ray?"

He smiles. "Y'know, guys'd pay top dollar for tips from a pro like me."

"Take it off the fourteen years' worth of birthday and Christmas gifts you owe me," I shoot back.

He looks a little taken aback; then his lips crinkle

into a smile. "I like how you do business, kid. C'mon, I need a smoke."

We go outside and settle on the front-porch steps. He sticks a cigarette in his mouth, lights up, takes a long drag, and gives me a sidelong glance. "All right. First, you need to lose the Linus look."

I glance down at my beige corduroys and orange-and-white-striped shirt.

"Those pants're way too big on you," he says, his cigarette bobbing up and down with each word. "Women like to see a man's ass and package, least a hint of it. And that shirt says, 'I watch *Benny Hill* and jerk off in a gym sock.'"

I love Benny Hill. *How'd he know? Howard and I have seen every episode.*

He sucks on his cigarette and blows smoke rings into the still air. "And what's with the 'do?"

"What about it?" I touch the back of my head.

He closes his eyes and shakes his head. "Carter's out of the White House. Time to enter the eighties."

Is this the reason girls don't go for me—because I'm a fashion disaster? I've always taken pride in what I wear, but what if I am totally out of it and don't know it? Suddenly I feel like Stanley Johnson, the greasy-headed geek in my class who wears corrective shoes and snorts when he laughs.

Uncle Ray mashes out his cigarette on the top step, flicks it into Mom's rosebushes, and rubs his hands together. "You got good raw material, kid. Revamp that look and go get 'em."

For the next hour, in front of the bathroom mirror, I experiment with my "'do." Mom has always cut my hair the same way, ever since I was in the first grade. I try watering down the cowlick in back, but it keeps popping up like a nerdy weed. I try parting my hair on the right, but the way it sweeps across my forehead, I resemble a pubescent Hitler. Parting it down the middle, I look like a loaf of Home Pride bread. Do I have "problem" hair? Will it doom me to the life of a virgin? Will I still be spending my nights with Mom watching Johnny Carson when I'm thirty? Are the African tribeswomen of *National Geographic* the only naked females I'll ever see? Is the Skin So Soft bottle the only—

"Les, darling!" I hear Mom call out from downstairs. "Time to wash up for supper!"

We all sit at the kitchen table eating Mom's chicken chow mein, a dish we have maybe once a year when company comes over. Is she trying to impress Uncle Ray? To appear more worldly? Dad's mood is soaring, thanks to Uncle Ray, who keeps refilling Dad's glass with red wine from a big jug marked Carlo Rossi. Mom, a devout teetotaler, frowns on Dad's rare instances of drinking, but Uncle Ray made a big deal about how he brought this expensive vintage Italian wine to celebrate the family reunion, and I can tell Mom feels she can't really say anything against it. I've never seen my father talk so much.

"Ray, can't tell you how good it is to have you back," Dad says, his speech a little slurry. "You know, just the other day I was thinking about that fly–fishing trip we took with Dad to Colorado back in '64."

Uncle Ray laughs and rolls his eyes. "Don't re-mind me."

I glance at Dad and Uncle Ray sitting beside each other. With the exception of their prominent Eckhardt brows, it's hard to believe they're brothers. Uncle Ray has a thick head of hair while Dad is balding, with patches of gray sticking out the sides. Trim and mus-cular, Uncle Ray looks as if he's spent every day of his life in the wind and sun; whereas Dad, who could rest his hands on his gut, looks as if he's spent the last twenty years working in a tunnel. Dad's wide–lapel brown Sears shirt makes him look all the more small-townish and out of it. Suddenly I feel a little guilty. Would Dad look more alive, more like Uncle Ray, if he didn't have to work so hard to provide for me and Mom?

"So there we were, at the top of Pikes Peak," Dad says with a beaming smile, "and the moment we all piled out of the car, it starts rolling backward."

Uncle Ray laughs and shakes his head. "The old man forgot to set the parking brake!"

"You should've seen the three of us running down

the mountain after that Plymouth," Dad laughs, his eyes tearing up.

Uncle Ray guffaws.

"The car shot right through the guardrail," Dad says as he pantomimes with his hands, "dropped a good hundred feet, and lands on top of a pine tree."

I laugh, although I've heard this story a hundred times. It's one of Dad's favorites. Mom produces a tepid smile while nibbling her chow mein. I notice she keeps looking at Uncle Ray out the corner of her eye.

"I never saw Dad so angry." Dad lifts his wineglass and wipes the corners of his eyes with the back of his hand.

Uncle Ray places his elbows on the table (something Mom never allows Dad and me to do) and leans forward. "He was angry 'cause he had no one to blame but himself."

Dad abruptly stops laughing.

"That's the thing about our old man," Uncle Ray says, suddenly serious. "He never could admit he made a mistake. Even that day. He claimed the parking brake was busted. I'm surprised he didn't blame the mountain."

A tense silence follows, and Mom places her fork on her plate. "Ray, we don't hear from you for what? Almost four years? And then, out of the blue, here you are."

Uh-oh. Here we go.

"Better late than never," Dad says, a little too quickly and jovially. "Honey, please pass the chow mein."

"Don't worry, Bev," Uncle Ray says. "I won't be in the way."

Mom shifts a little in her chair, as if digging in for battle, and asks, "Are you still playing guitar in that rock 'n' roll band?"

"Nope. Y'know, we stood a real shot at landing a contract with a big label," Uncle Ray says, "till our lead singer died."

"How?" Dad asks.

"ODed on Freon," Uncle Ray says, and sips his wine.

"Freon?!" Dad asks, horrified. "How does someone overdose on Freon?"

"Sniffed it from a pressurized can. Lungs froze instantly. Died right on top of a groupie."

Mom and Dad exchange a concerned look; then Mom clears her throat and says, "Let's see now." She glances at the ceiling as if there's a list written up there. "Before the band you were an actor, if I'm not mistaken, and before that you were a blackjack dealer in Las Vegas."

"Don't forget I sold Porsches in Arizona...."

"Why, Ray, I guess you're a jack-of-all-trades," Mom concludes.

Uncle Ray grins and winks at Mom. "And, yes, Bev, a master of none. But if you're gonna apply a cliché to me, I'd rather you go with 'a rolling stone.' No moss on me."

It's so cool the way Uncle Ray handles Mom's

jabs—he just won't let her get to him. He pulls his red duffel bag onto his lap and unzips it. "Have a little something for each of you."

"Oh now, you didn't have to go and do that," Dad says.

Uncle Ray removes an antique toy airplane from the bag, hands it to Dad, and says, "I realize I'm only about thirty years late on this."

Dad breaks out in a wide grin as he marvels at the plane. "Ray, you son of a gun. Why, it's the spitting image—where'd you find it?"

"Wasn't easy, let me tell ya."

Dad turns to Mom and me. "When I was a boy— around seven—my favorite toy was a model B-52, just like this one. Well, one day I did something that really irked Ray and he smashed it with a brick, just flattened the thing...."

"And I haven't heard the end of it since," Uncle Ray says. "Till now, hopefully."

"I couldn't be happier, little brother. Couldn't be happier."

Hearing Dad and Uncle Ray talk about the old days makes me wish I had a brother or a sister I could one day share growing-up stories with.

Uncle Ray reaches back into his bag as he turns to me. "Your old man tells me you're kind of an expert on magic." Out comes a thick old book with HOUDINI's SECRETS pressed into the tattered black binding.

"Thanks," I say, trying to sound excited about receiving an old book.

"Oh, wait, there's one other thing." He lifts a dark-brown leather jacket, with a sheepskin fleece lining, from the bag. "It's a genuine bomber from World War II. Hope it fits."

"It's awesome!" I say, tugging it on. "Thanks, Uncle Ray. Gonna go see how it looks!" I race into the bathroom and model it in front of the mirror for several minutes. I *love* the way it looks on me, with its worn, lived-in leather. Then I notice a white tag hanging from the bottom button: "$350." I can't believe Uncle Ray has spent so much. Is he rich? If so, why is he staying on my bottom bunk?

When I return to the table, Mom is holding a small black-satin box, and Uncle Ray nods. "Go on, open it."

She does, and I watch her mouth fall open as she removes a bronze pin set with a red jewel.

"It's English," Uncle Ray says. "From the 1880s."

Mom shakes her head, quickly returns the brooch to the box, and hands it back. "I—no, Ray, I cannot accept this."

"Well, why not?" Uncle Ray laughs, as if it's the most ludicrous thing he's ever heard.

"It's far too . . . too extravagant," Mom says. "You shouldn't have done this."

"Don't be silly," Dad chimes in. "You deserve it, Bev."

"I won't take it back," Uncle Ray adds.

"Well, then, it'll just have to remain on this table." Mom gets to her feet and starts collecting the dishes. "Les, please help me clear the table."

"Ray, you've got to see my new radio transceiver," Dad says quickly. "Tallest antenna in town. Why, last night I talked with a fellow in South Africa—"

"Uh, Dad," I interrupt, "the Chinese vanishing box...?"

"Not tonight, son." He turns back to Uncle Ray. "Anyway, that South African man sounded like he was right next door, the reception was that clear."

An hour later I'm lying on my bunk watching Uncle Ray—in pressed black jeans and dark-blue silk shirt— blow-dry, mousse, and sculpt his hair into cool-guy perfection.

I study him carefully, making mental notes.

"Uncle Ray, out of all the places you've been," I ask, "which has the hottest women?"

"Australia. No question about it. They're all tanned knockouts down there. And here's the best part: they go topless on the beaches."

"Get outta here!" My voice totally breaks.

"Swear to God. Imagine the most gorgeous chicks in the world just walking in G-strings with their breasts hanging out. I'm telling you, it's heaven on earth. You gotta see it for yourself. Maybe I'll take you Down Under someday."

"You mean it?"

"Sure, kid, why not?" He snatches his pack of Pall Malls and his alligator-skin wallet from the dresser, stuffing them into his pocket.

"Where you going?"

"Gonna see if the hometown remembers ol' Ray." He turns and winks at me. "'Night, kid."

I wait until I hear his Corvette thunder to life and squeal off before I shut the door and lock it. I know what I'm about to do isn't right. I check his dresser drawers first, but they contain nothing but his boxer shorts, socks, and a carton of Pall Malls. At the closet I pull out his overstuffed suitcase, set it on the floor, and try to open it, but it's padlocked. Then I notice his duffel bag. I unzip it and see, in the bottom, a color photograph of a naked dark-skinned lady reclining on a sofa and smiling at the camera. I blink. Wowza! She is beyond hot: her long black, curly hair cascades around her naked boobies! And she's smiling a perfect toothpaste-ad smile. A small silver ring protrudes from her belly button. One leg is draped over the side of the sofa—I can see her pubic hair! It's a thin, manicured little strip of fur. Women shave *down there*?

There are dozens of pictures of her in various positions—all naked, all fantastic.

And right here in Mom's house! In my very room! It's like I found a secret passage to the Playboy Mansion. And to think that for the past two years

I've been getting off on bra ads from nursing-supply catalogs.

Is this Uncle Ray's girlfriend? Can he introduce me?

Dear Jesus . . . I know I said I wasn't going to jerk off for an entire week, but You know I wasn't expecting to find those pictures. I'll try to control myself better next time and not look at those pictures ever again. I hope You can forgive me. In Your Name. Amen.

As I return the pictures to the duffel bag, I see, at the bottom, a shining metallic curve sticking out of a small black towel. Carefully I unwrap it.

The chrome-plated revolver fits perfectly in my palm, and there is a dusting of black—gunpowder?—on the nicked barrel. Glancing back into the bag, I see several stubby cartridges. Could this be the gun that killed that nightclub owner? A chill shimmies up my spine.

Then, from the floor vent, I hear my mother's voice: "Roger! Just what do you think you're doing?"

I move closer to the vent and hear my father's slurred reply: "Thought maybe you'd like to, y'know . . ."

"You are drunk, sir," she says.

"Oh, c'mon, honey, it's been so long since we've done it."

"For heaven's sake, Roger, don't be silly. Now just go to sleep."

I step back. I've never heard my parents make love, or even talk about sex in any way whatsoever. Strange and conflicted emotions bubble up inside me. Part of me is totally grossed out. And part of me is sort of happy for them—they're normal, they have urges like I do, or at least Dad does. But he sounds so lonely and deprived, and Mom was so cold.

"Les!" Mom calls from the bottom of the stairs.

I quickly return the gun to the duffel bag.

"Time for Johnny Carson!" she yells.

"Not tonight!" I yell back. "Too tired."

She denies Dad. I'll deny her.

The last time I look at the digital bedside alarm clock, it's almost two a.m. and Uncle Ray still isn't home.

Seduction Tip Number 3:

Developing Your Sex Sense

The Seductive Man has a superbly developed
tactile sense. To develop your faculties, gather
together the following items: a piece of toast,
a large marshmallow, a silk handkerchief, and a
tomato. Lay them out on a table and strip to
the waist. With your eyes closed, slowly touch
each item, then rub it on your body. *Remember*
how each item feels. Repeat this exercise until
each one's unique texture imprints itself on
your fingers and skin.

The next morning at school I find it difficult to concentrate or to look any female in the eye. Who in my very

own school is shaved down there? What makes a girl decide to shave or not? Is it just a matter of taste? Like how a girl styles her hair? Or is it a—a health thing? What does Charity Conners do?

Keeping myself concealed is my biggest challenge this morning. By lunchtime I'm desperate for relief. So, while everyone is in the cafeteria innocently eating cabbage biscuits and peach cobbler, I sneak into the empty and dark gymnasium and stuff some napkins into my underwear. A double check to make sure I'm alone, then I proceed to the corner where the climbing rope dangles. Hoisting myself onto the thick cotton-and-hemp cord, I press my thighs together and strain to pull myself up.

Up and down, up and down. That familiar warm, intense, and intoxicating pulsing starts, and then I hear: "Eckhardt?!"

I twist around and look down at Coach Turkle framed in the doorway, his beefy hands on his hips. "What the hell're you doing?"

"Uh, hey, Coach." God, my voice is so warbly. "I was just . . . practicing."

"You know better than to be in here without supervision."

I ease myself to the floor as Coach Turkle approaches. "Practicing, huh? I like to hear that, Eckhardt." He pulls on the rope, as if making sure it's secure. "Y'know, rope climbing is a terrific full-body workout, and it could save your life someday, too. Tell ya what, I got some time right now, let me show you a few things."

"Coach, you don't have—"

He reaches out, handing me the rope. "Go on now."

I moan inwardly.

"The rope needs to go between your legs like so," he says as he threads it around my knees and back between the insteps of my sneakers.

My hands burn, my arms are shaking.

"Now clamp your feet together."

I do, discovering that when I support my weight with my feet, my arms no longer shake.

"When you clamp your feet like that, it functions as a brake, freeing up your hands and arms," he says. "Now, I want you to start inchworming yourself up: bend your legs, loosen the brake with your feet, and pull yourself up about a foot. Let's see you do it."

My heart pumps and my arms strain, but it isn't too painful—tough, but manageable. Soon I have climbed higher than I've ever been. I glance down and feel dizzy, seeing how small Coach looks.

"You got it!" he says. "Remember to bend those legs."

Looking up, I can't believe I'm a mere few feet from the red line that marks the Monkey Club.

"Go on up to that line, Les! You can do it!"

My arms are starting to shake again. I think I feel a hernia forming.

"You're almost there!" he yells. "Take a breather, then do one more big pull!"

I inhale deeply and heave myself up. Suddenly my nose is touching the red line. Coach claps and cheers. "You did it, Les! You did it!"

I cling to the rope, catching my breath and laughing. I have done the impossible! Only the most in-shape jocks make it to the Monkey Club.

"Now inchworm your way down—slow and steady," Coach orders. "Just do the reverse of what I showed you."

When my sneakers touch the mat, I'm breathless but feeling really good. This is the most working out I've done in years, or ever. Coach Turkle pumps my hot and tingly right hand.

"You're stronger than you think, Eckhardt," he says. "A little more refinement of your technique and we'll have you clambering up to that ceiling like a three-toed monkey. What do you say I meet you in here to-morrow, same time?"

"Uh, okay."

"See you then." He cuffs my shoulder before am-bling out of the gymnasium.

I collapse on the mat, my chest heaving from laugh-ter. Who knew? What else could this Monkey Boy do?

"Fact—or fallacy?" asks Howard. "The human eyeball moves one hundred times per second."

"Fact, but only when Charity Conners walks by," I quip.

Side by side we're coasting down Walnut Street on our bikes while balancing Frosty Queen milk shakes.

"Fact—or fallacy?" Howard continues. "Kangaroos have been sighted in North America—"

"Hey, Leth–bian!"

Shit-shit-shit. I begin trembling all over. Brett's bike pulls up on my right. Misty, his skeletal stoner girl–friend, all long black hair and pale yellow roots, shares the banana seat with him.

"Aw, look, Little Lord Leth–bian and hith lard–ath butt buddy are on a date." Brett reaches over, snatching the shake from my hand. He takes a long suck, then hurls the cup.

"Thanks a lot, Brett," I say.

Brett glares at Howard and growls.

"I, uh, suddenly remember something I have to do," Howard says, his voice quavering, as he turns and dis–appears down a side street.

Dear Jesus . . . how about a lightning bolt through Brett's head about now, huh?

"Y'know why I hate'th ya, Leth–bian?" Brett rams his front wheel into mine. I keep control of the weaving handlebars until I hit the curb and catapult onto a lawn.

I clamber to my feet, only to be met by Brett's fist in my gut. Landing hard on my butt, I feel as if I'm going to vomit. Brett's shadow falls over me.

"I hate'th ya 'cauthe your dad'th a rich doctor and you're an ugly faggot," he says, and shoves me down.

"C'mon, don't hurt him, Brett!" Misty pleads.

"Shut up, bitch!"

He body-slams me, his full weight crashing into my midsection and knocking the air from my chest. A million little white dots swirl in front of my eyes, and the earth feels like it's pitching. I lie waiting for oxygen to refill my lungs when I hear a rumbling car engine and the squealing of brakes.

"What the hell?!"

I sit up on my elbows and watch Uncle Ray hop out of his Corvette and charge over to Brett, who jumps to his feet and raises his hands. "No harm done, thir, no harm done."

Uncle Ray violently grabs Brett by his shirt collar, gets in his face, and hisses, "You so much as sneeze in his direction again and I'll reach into your ugly mouth and pull your asshole up through your throat. You understand me, you worthless piece of shit?" Brett, who is on his tiptoes, nods vehemently, his butt-ugly face the color of milk.

"Now fuck off while you can still walk!" Uncle Ray releases Brett, who scrambles to his bike and tears off, Misty chasing after him and yelling, "Hey, wait up!"

Uncle Ray extends his hand, pulling me to my feet. "You gonna let him get away with that?"

"C'mon, you saw how big he is!"

"He bullies you 'cause you let him," he says. "One

good blow to the tip of his nose and he'll leave you alone."

"Yeah, but first I'll get killed."

"Not if you do it right."

Uncle Ray holds up his flattened hand. "Make a fist and hit me with all you've got."

"Look, Uncle Ray, in case you haven't noticed, I'm not exactly the physical type."

"You're perfectly capable, just need to develop your upper-body strength. Now shut up and hit me!"

I punch him as hard as I can. *Ouch.*

"You call that a punch? Try it again. C'mon, faster and harder."

So I hit again.

"Faster!"

I fire away, remembering what Coach Turkle said earlier today: "You're stronger than you think, Eckhardt."

Uncle Ray drops his hand. "Not bad. You have potential, kid."

I blink at Uncle Ray a moment. "You serious?"

"I've known a hundred guys like that idiot. The only thing they respect is pain. If you want him to leave you alone, you gotta take no prisoners. C'mon, let's put your bike in the trunk."

I've never ridden in a convertible before. It's low to the ground. The leather seat feels good against my legs, and the wind whips my hair as the sun blasts my upturned face. Used to riding in my mom's high-up Buick, I feel as if I'm sitting in the cockpit of a jet fighter. I gaze in awe at the glass-covered dials of the instrument panel and the big black-and-white fuzzy dice dangling from the rearview mirror. With his right hand on the marble-like blue-and-white gearshift, Uncle Ray, sitting way back in his seat, steers with just his left index finger. If I had this car, I know I could land Charity. I sit up tall so everyone can see me.

"Didn't your old man ever teach you how to defend yourself?" Uncle Ray asks as he heads out of town on Tripp Street.

"This is Doctor Dad we're talking about."

"I know for a fact that your dad was taught how to use his dukes. When you do retaliate, try to do it in front of that moron's girlfriend or his buddies—maximize the humiliation. Remember, take no prisoners."

Uncle Ray downshifts and spins the wheel to the left, pulling into the Frosty Queen and Sleep Inn Motel lot. In front of the café he switches off the engine and turns to me. "Have a favor to ask you."

"Sure."

In a low voice he says, "If anyone you don't know should ask about me, tell them you haven't seen me and you don't know where I am. Got it?"

"Why? Are you the Kansas City killer?" It shoots out of my mouth before I realize it.

Uncle Ray looks at me a moment—perhaps startled, but it's hard to tell behind those Ray-Bans—then grins. "Yeah, I'm a killer all right."

I swallow hard. *Okay, he isn't the Kansas City killer.*

"C'mon, Magnum, P.I." He opens his door. "I'll buy you a Coke."

The Frosty Queen is thick with grease and cigarette smoke. A couple of farmers in seed caps hunch at the counter. On the juke Waylon Jennings twangs on about Luckenbach, Texas—Waylon and Willie, and the boys. A hot young waitress with blond hair and bright green eyes sashays on over.

Uncle Ray smiles his killer smile. "Well, well, well."

She grins a little self-consciously.

"Shelleby, is it?" Uncle Ray says, referring to the name tag resting on her right boob. "Now, I bet there's a fascinating story behind that name."

Her smile widens as she gathers the menus from the counter. I see she's wearing a wedding ring. "My mom wanted to name me Shelby, but Daddy wanted Shelley. So, they just combined 'em."

"Shel-le-by. A girl so nice they named her twice."

She blushes. "Just you two?"

"Yes, Shelleby, Eckhardt party of two," Uncle Ray says in a pompous voice. "My secretary made reservations for four o'clock."

"Secretary?" she asks.

"Wait," Uncle Ray says, "isn't this Spago?"

"Yeah, and I'm Christie Brinkley." She rolls her eyes good-naturedly and shows us to a corner table. "What can I get you two to drink?"

"I'm just having coffee. Les, what would you like?"

"Dr Pepper, please."

Shelleby collects our menus and heads toward the counter. Uncle Ray's eyes linger on her butt and he shakes his head. "Mmm–mm sweet."

"God, Uncle Ray. Wish I could talk to women like you do."

"Now why can't you?"

I shrug. "I always get nervous."

"Nervous about what?"

I laugh in an "isn't it obvious?" way. "Being turned down."

"Kid, I've been turned down more times than a sheet at the Motel 6."

"You have?"

He nods. "But I can live with rejection 'cause I know it's just one less 'no' I have to hear before I get a 'yes.' Law of averages, law of the jungle.

"If you let the fear of being turned down stop you from pursuing chicks, you might as well throw in the towel right now." Uncle Ray leans in close, his elbows on the table, as if he was about to share a deep secret. "Most guys sit around with their thumbs up their asses waiting to hear back from one woman—or worse, they wait around for a woman to hit on them! Big mistake. You have to be constantly pursuing. Like a shark. For every five women I hit on, I get maybe one phone number."

"Yeah, well, I'm not outgoing like you." I'm disgusted by how self–pitying I sound.

"Then ya just gotta force yourself to be."

Shelleby returns with the coffee and Dr Pepper.

"Why, Shelleby, honey," Uncle Ray says, "what're you doing working in this fry bin? You belong on film with those peepers of yours."

She blushes again, clearly trying to keep her composure. "Will that be all?"

"For now," Uncle Ray says, very suggestively.

Shelleby sashays off, and I glance out the window as the Trailways bus hisses to a stop (a wooden bench under the Frosty's awning composes the Harker City bus depot).

"You have to be willing to walk up to a perfect stranger and strike up a conversation," Uncle Ray says, "like I did with that Shelleby."

"But what do I say?"

"It's not what you say, it's how you say it—with your eyes, your posture, your verve."

"What's 'verve'?"

Scanning the room, Uncle Ray reaches into his jacket pocket and removes a small silver flask. He unscrews the top, pours a brownish liquid into his coffee, and stirs. Up till now I have never seen a flask except in old movies on TV.

"Most morons see a woman they're attracted to and instantly pull back 'cause they don't want to make a mistake," he says between sips of coffee. "Chicks smell fear in a guy like a hound smells coon. Makes the guy look weak and unmanly. Window of opportunity closed. So it's crucial that the moment you see a babe, within seconds, you say hello. Make it a knee-jerk reaction. Women like fearless guys. Fearless guys get laid."

"Did you know all this when you lived in Harker City? Or is it something you picked up on the road?"

He settles back and tastes more coffee. "I once had a friend, Joey. He was the master. Bald, kinda pudgy. But he got laid left and right. I watched him operate. Taught me it's not what you have but how you present it. The rest I learned from the school of hard knockers." He laughs at his own joke.

I sip my Dr Pepper. Cool and fizzy and sweet. Dad always warns me that soda pop is nothing but pure sugar that'll rot your teeth and turn to fat.

"Y'see how I made a little joke? Humor's vital—puts the lady at ease. And notice how I asked her about her name. Try to find something unique or personal—usually it's a piece of jewelry or clothing—and ask her the story behind it. Questions are the best way to get chicks to open up and tell you intimate details about themselves."

"Sounds complicated."

"Not really."

"You have a steady girlfriend, Uncle Ray?" I casually inquire, hoping he'll divulge something about the naked woman.

"Hell, no. I never tie myself down. My life's too damn short." He takes a big slug of coffee, sets the cup on the saucer, and wipes his lips with a napkin. "Now—you got all that? Remember, fearless guys get laid."

I affirm it and nod vigorously, already planning my next move with Charity.

"I'll be damned," a baritone voice booms from across the room.

A tall bearded man in blue coveralls and a cap saying LEO's CONCRETE lumbers to our table and sticks out his boxing glove of a hand. "It's been a real long time, Ray."

Uncle Ray stands and shakes the man's hand. "Why, Big Leo, how you been?"

"I'm good, I'm good." The man turns his head, calling over his shoulder, "Shelleby, come over here! Want you to meet an old buddy of mine!"

She shuffles over, coffeepot in hand, and Big Leo wraps his massive arm around her shoulders. "Honey, this here's Ray Eckhardt. We used to stir up trouble together in high school. Ray, this is my wife, Shelleby."

Uncle Ray smiles and says, "It's a pleasure to meet you, Shelleby."

Guess this means Shelleby's one less conquest for Uncle Ray.

Seduction Tip Number 4:

Pelvis Power

Grip the back of a straight–back chair, keeping your feet about twenty inches apart. Steadily thrust your pelvis forward and back twenty times. Now, in the forward–thrust position, rotate your hips slightly. Forward–rotate–back! Forward–rotate–back! Do this for ten minutes a day. Not only will this strengthen your lower back muscles, it will enable you to penetrate deep within her.

The next morning I get up extra early. Wash, mousse, blow–dry, and sculpt my hair using Uncle Ray's utensils and technique.

When I debut my creation in the kitchen, Mom sets down her spatula. "What happened to you?"

"It's my new look," I announce.

"According to experts at the Centers for Disease Control," Dad says from the table, his face buried in the newspaper, "a new strain of chicken flu could wipe out a quarter of the U.S. population by the year 2000."

"Well, I don't know," Mom says, staring at my hair. "It looks wet. Makes me want to take a towel to you."

"I'm running late, Mom," I say, snatching a piece of toast from the toaster. "See you tonight."

"A boy needs a good breakfast!"

At school, striding toward my locker, I instantly sense that girls are checking me out.

"Ah, the new hairdo," Howard says as he approaches my locker. "The signal to the females, a beacon that announces, 'I am a contender. Date bait. One juicy piece of man meat.'"

"I'm not speaking to you," I say to my books.

"Can't say that I blame you," he admits. "I know I shouldn't have run off when Brett showed up yesterday. It's just—ever since he broke my nose, the guy scares the shit out of me."

"How do you think *I* feel?"

"I'm sorry," he says, and sounds like he means it.

Whack! I feel a hand slap the top of my head. Brett

walks past, making pouting lips. "No one'th gonna thave you nekth time, Leth–bian."

In the cafeteria I maneuver my way right in front of Charity Conners in the lunch line. As I stand there waiting to be served, molded–plastic pastel tray in hand, I swallow hard and take a deep breath.

Dear Jesus . . . don't let me screw this up! I won't jerk off for a year or ever look at that naked woman's pictures ever again. Amen.

Sweating a little, I turn and face her. She looks at me with those swimming–pool–blue eyes. *Hold it together, Les. Just say something.* I manage a smile and an al–most knee–jerk "hi."

She raises a curious eyebrow.

"Hi," I say again, still smiling at her, still maintaining eye contact.

"Hi." She doesn't sound pissed off or annoyed.

"I . . . like your earrings," I say, my voice very shaky.

"Thanks."

"Are they Chinese?"

Chinese? Where the hell did I get Chinese? Gotta stick to the script, Les.

I am feeling light–headed.

"I don't know what they are," she says, and touches her right earring. "I bought 'em at a flea market."

"That's so cool."

What to say next? What to say next? Questions!

"Uh, which flea market?"

"It was in downtown St. Louis."

"That's so cool." *Stop saying "so cool."*

I'm out of questions. Time for my much-rehearsed joke. I look around, as if lost. "Wait, my secretary was supposed to Spago for make our reservations this dump."

Goddamn it!

She gives me a confused look.

" 'Wait, my secretary was supposed to make our reservation for Spago, not this dump' is what I meant to say before I had that little stroke."

She cracks up! A full guffaw. But is she laughing *at* me?

I offer my hand. "I'm Les."

"Oh, I remember you, Booger."

"Excuse me?"

"You're Booger. That's what all us girls called you behind your back in fifth grade."

I clear my throat. "You, uh, did?"

"You were always picking your nose and wiping it on the bottom of your desk."

"That wasn't me." *God, she does remember me.*

"Yes it was. You sat right beside me. And before I moved, you once called me Turkey Tits."

"Well... I'm real sorry about that."

"I hold no grudges. Besides, it was kind of funny."

She glances at my extended hand, to make sure there are no boogers?

"Don't worry," I say. "I've graduated from Nose Picker Rehab. Have a diploma and everything."

She grins and accepts my clammy paw. "Charity."

"Charity. Now, that's a wholly original name. I bet there's a story behind that."

"Not really. Mom just liked the sound of it."

"Well, I like it, too," I declare, but can't bring myself to say "a beautiful name for a beautiful woman." So I say, "Must be tough coming back to little ol' Harker City after St. Louis."

She shrugs. "It's an adjustment, but I'm surviving." I'm hypnotized by the movement of her sumptuous lips. *Oh God, I feel a boner forming. Quick, think of Great-aunt Irma.*

"Look, you're up," she says.

"Huh?" I say, petrified.

With a tilt of her head she motions behind me. The hairnetted lunch ladies stand waiting for me, their plastic–gloved hands clutching their big spoons.

"Well, nice to see you again, Charity."

"That's Turkey Tits to you, Booger."

So . . . she's funny, a funny girl. And I have completed step one. I turn around as peas and carrots and funky–looking meat are deposited onto my tray.

"Eckhardt?!" Coach Turkle stands in the doorway, hands on his hips. "Meet me in the gym in ten minutes."

***

Coach is standing on the mat next to the rope when I step into the gym. He rubs his hands together. "All right, climber, let's go."

I grab hold of the rope, weave it between my legs, and start to inchworm my way up. It is a lot harder than yesterday, and my arms begin to burn. I drop to the floor.

"What the heck happened?" he asks.

"Look, Coach, I appreciate what you're trying to do—"

"You just get back on up there."

"But I'm just not the athletic type. . . ."

I suddenly remember what Uncle Ray said about my being perfectly capable, and how I need to develop my upper-body strength. I grip the rope again. It is a painful, awful climb, and I only make it about halfway to the Monkey Club line.

"This is as far as I can go," I say, breathless, swinging and looking down at Coach.

He crosses his arms at his chest. "To the line, Eckhardt."

"I can't, Coach."

"To the line!"

"But I'm on lunch break!"

"To the line!"

I heave myself up three times. *Sa-dis-tic ass-hole.*

Sa-dis-tic ass-hole. Sa-dis-tic ass-hole. My nose hits the mark. "There! Happy?!" I yell.

"See ya tomorrow," he says on his way out of the gym. "Same time."

After school I pedal home fast. Can't wait to tell Uncle Ray about my Charity encounter. I also can't wait to get advice on what my next move should be. But when I arrive home, his Corvette isn't in the drive. I ride downtown but there's no sign of him there, either. I cruise past the Frosty Queen and, sure enough, his Corvette is parked right by the door. I rest my bike against the side of the rusty building and go in. The place is empty except for Carla Smith, the yellow-haired waitress, who leans against the counter watching Phil Donahue on the TV above the pie case.

"Lookin' for your uncle, Les?" Carla asks.

"He come in here?"

She laughs a sarcastic laugh and says to the TV, "Yeah, he came in here all right."

I look around again to make sure he isn't in a booth or something. "He in the bathroom?"

She motions me over with her pudgy index finger and says quietly, "He and Mrs. Hotpants decided to check themselves into a room out back."

I know it's wrong. Really wrong. And kinda disgusting. And yet part of me is in awe—my very own uncle is a real man of action. A fearless guy.

At home I wait for Uncle Ray in Dad's La-Z-Boy while watching *The Addams Family*. Hmm ... maybe Howard *does* have a point: Lurch and Thing *don't* seem to ever appear in the same room together.

It's not until almost an hour later, during *Hogan's Heroes*, that Uncle Ray moseys through the back door, his Hawaiian shirt unbuttoned practically to his belly button.

"Hey," he says as he walks past me. The breeze that follows him reeks of sweat and flowery perfume. He flops on the sofa. "That bully bother you again?"

"Kinda."

He sits up. "Come over here and let's work on that punch."

For the next few minutes Uncle Ray coaches me on how to throw a right hook. "Plant your feet and throw all your weight into the punch. Use your whole body. Be fast. In and out. Like lightning. Remember to punch past your target." He punches the air, demonstrating. "Hit just above the tip of the nose for maximum impact. All right, let's see you do it."

He holds up his hand and I punch it. My arms are sore from the rope climbing.

"Wait a minute." Uncle Ray drops his hand and

squeezes my upper right arm. "You been lifting weights?"

"You can tell?"

He nods. "Your arm's tighter. Stick with it and you'll have that jerk begging your forgiveness."

I resume pounding his open hand and say, "Got up the guts to talk to Charity today. What do you think my next move should be?"

"Know where she lives?"

"Yeah, over by the water tower."

"Got a leash?"

Taking Uncle Ray's advice ("Chicks can't resist a guy with a dog. She'll think you're a good guy, a guy she'd like to be with"), I leash up my overweight, arthritic, blind-in-one-eye beagle, Rusty, and we light out. Rusty, who hasn't been out of the backyard in years, makes several stops to catch his breath and empty his bladder. Lately I've overhead Mom and Dad whispering about putting ol' Rusty "to sleep," but I'll never let that happen and they know it. I will take care of Rusty until his last stale dog breath is exhaled. He'd do the same for me.

About twenty years later we make it to Charity's. She lives in a sky-blue two-story clapboard with a white wraparound front porch and a gigantic yellow wooden butterfly affixed to the garage. As Rusty and I nonchalantly stroll past, I notice the front door is open behind the screen door, and I hear some kind of organ music from inside. Rusty stops right in front of her house. And squats.

Aw, Rus, do you have to do this here? Right now?

"Dropping off some fertilizer?"

Charity is walking down the sidewalk toward us, that huge magazine curled in her hand. My pulse accelerates.

"Oh, hi," I say, hurriedly stepping in front of Rusty.

"Hey, Booger."

I really wish she'd stop calling me that.

"Name's Les."

She looks down and grins at Rusty as he performs the slowest bowel movement in history.

"What's your dog's name?"

"Rusty."

"Hiya, Rusty."

He looks up at her, howls a little, and continues his pained efforts.

God, Rus, how long does it take you?

"How old is he?"

"Fourteen."

"My friend in St. Louis had a cat who lived to be twenty."

"I like cats, too," I say. "But my mom's allergic. You, uh, live around here?"

She points at the blue house, where the organ music crescendos.

"With the phantom of the opera?"

She smiles. "That's my grandmother. She's organist at the Our Redeemer Lutheran Church."

"Tell your grandma I'm sorry about Rusty's contribution to her lawn." I motion to the big magazine in her hand. "Got cataracts or something?"

She laughs. "No, it's just big. Andy Warhol, the pop artist, puts it out, so it's kinda out there."

Rusty finally finishes and, with his hind legs, starts kicking dirt onto his creation. Charity crouches down and pets him. *Time to make your move, Les. But first a silent prayer:*

Dear Jesus ... it's been three days since I've been with the Skin So Soft bottle—a record. Keeping this in mind, please make Charity say yes. In Your loving Name. Amen."

"Charity?"

She lifts those blues to me.

"Would you, uh, want to go bowling with me Friday night?"

There is a long pause; then a smile curls the corners of her mouth and she says, sounding genuinely excited, "I'd love to."

Thank you, Jesus! Thank you!

"Great," I say smoothly, utterly nonchalant. "I'll come by your place, say, seven o'clock?"

"It's a date."

A date! She said it was a "date." I'm officially going on a date with Charity Conners! This is the greatest moment of my life.

I want to kiss and squeeze her, but I sense that would be too much, too forward. I shake the dirt and grass from my jeans and say, "Friday night, then."

"Friday night, Booger."

Thank You! Thank You! Thank You!

Seduction Tip Number 5:
Lip Service

To develop Seductive–Man sensitivity in your
lips, purchase a baby bottle. Now close your eyes
and place the rubber nipple on your moistened
lips (your lips should never be dry or rough!).
Keeping in mind a woman's nipples are a very
sensitive erogenous zone, slowly run the nipple
along your lips from side to side. Now knead it
with your lips. Ever so lightly caress and twirl it
with your tongue. Never apply too much
pressure. Practice daily.

The next twenty–four hours are a blur. I'm too ecstatic
to concentrate on anything. When people speak to me,

their words sound like the *wha-wha*speak of adults in a *Peanuts* cartoon. I feel utterly validated. I have a date. I'm someone. I float through the halls of my school with a grin that won't leave. When I pass Charity, I say, "See you tonight," and she smiles and nods. I imagine my life with her as my girlfriend. Oh, the places we'll go.... The stuff we'll do to each other.

But as the day wears on, I melt into fear. How am I supposed to behave on a date? What do I talk about? Am I expected to kiss her? I don't know how to kiss a real girl. I suddenly want to cancel and stay home and practice magic tricks until it's time to watch Johnny Carson with my mom.

"Eckhardt, you look like you swallowed a toad," Howard says to me at the lunch table. "You okay?"

I push my untouched plate of Salisbury steak away and glance at Charity, who is lunching at a table with two other girls. Coach Turkle appears in the doorway behind her and motions me into the gym with a jerk of his buzz-cut, anvil-shaped head. I shake my head. He motions again, turns, and walks out.

"Not today, Coach," I say as I shuffle into the gym, my Nikes squeaking on the rubbery floor. "I don't feel so hot."

He pulls on the rope. "Unless you got somethin' fatal, hop to it!" His voice echoes in the cavernous space.

I stop about five feet from the rope and say, "I'm

going to level with you, Coach. It's very nice you're trying to help me and all, but I just don't want to do this
anymore. So, thanks anyway."

"Son, I know damn well you weren't trying to exercise when I came in here that first day and caught you
on the rope," he says. "I've been teaching phys ed for
fifteen years. I know all about boys and ropes."

I shake my head, even as my flaming face be-
trays me.

"You're all revved up like an eight-cylinder Chevy
on high-octane with no place to burn rubber," he says.
"Testosterone can drive a boy insane—I've seen it.
'Course there's no replacement for self-gratification,
but you can't exactly do that at school, now can ya?"

Coach Turkle, who never seems to care about anything but his beloved football players, is talking to me
about jerking off. This is simply unbelievable.

"Way I see it, working out channels that energy," he
says. "Takes the edge off, clears the mind. Now, you
give me fifteen minutes every day till the end of the
school year, and I guarantee you'll feel a helluva lot
more relaxed, and that'll make you more confident
with the girls. That's what you want, right?"

Not only do I climb the rope to the Monkey Club
three times, I do twenty push-ups and forty sit-ups.
Thanks, Coach!

***

"Think of the first date as a reconnaissance mission," Uncle Ray says. Seated in my desk chair, in nothing but his black silk boxer shorts, he curls a barbell in his right hand. "Don't plan on getting lucky tonight. On this date you just want to gather information."

Okay, I can do that. I'll be like a detective. I'll be Magnum, P.I.

"Where you taking her?" he asks.

"Bowling."

He shakes his head as he switches the weight to his left hand.

"What!" I say. "This is Harker City. I'm limited."

"A bowling alley is not romantic. What's this chick like?"

"Well, she's tall, with short black hair—"

"No, I mean, what's she *like*? A cheerleader? Bookish?"

"I guess you'd say she's the artistic type."

"Artistic type? In Harker City? Kid, you're striking out left and right. Okay. So, wear black and take her for a walk in a cemetery. And don't wear cologne. And don't comb your hair! Freak chicks go for the messy-haired type.

"Then, when you first see her tonight, tell her how good she looks," he continues, and switches hands again. "Even the freaky ones love to hear that."

"What do we talk about?"

"Too many guys waste the first date on chitchat or trying to be funny. And don't—I repeat, don't—talk about yourself! Remember, your objective is to find out what turns *her* on. So, first you'll need to know if she's a milk–chocolate type or a dark–chocolate type."

"Huh?"

"Ask her if she prefers milk chocolate or dark chocolate. Have both on hand."

"How will that help?"

"If she goes for the milk chocolate, then she's the old–fashioned romantic type," he explains. "She'll require flowers and love notes before you'll get her bra off. The dark–chocolate types are more aggressive and edgy. They like guys who will challenge them in some way. Be prepared to have some deep, passionate conversations about life and death with the dark–chocolate kind."

"What if she doesn't like any kind of chocolate?"

"What woman doesn't like chocolate? Next, you gotta find out her other interests. What's her favorite food? Does she like Sting or Billy Joel? Try to be casual and romantic in your questioning. Remember, you'll use all this information on setting up the next date."

"This is a lot to remember."

"Right. So, Les, keep the date short. Always leave 'em wanting more." He smiles at me and sets the barbell on the floor. "You'll do fine, kid."

Will I?

***

"You're awfully dressed up for going over to Howard's," Mom says as she places the IGA circular and scissors on the kitchen table. From down the hall I hear the crackle of Dad's ham radio.

"Well, I, uh, got to thinking," I say. "The parsonage is an extension of the church, so I should look more formal when I go over there, right?"

"I suppose so, but black is so, well, morbid. Anyway, tell the reverend hello and be home by nine, dear."

On my bike ride to Charity's my heart keeps flip-flopping and I'm sweating so profusely that my shirt sticks to my chest and back like plastic wrap. My carefully sculpted hair is a punctured soufflé by the time I turn onto her street. Charity is sitting on the front porch, petting a cat curled around her left ankle. I hear the organ music coming from inside the house.

"Hi there," I say as I hop off and put down the kickstand.

She looks up, smiling her stellar smile. "Booger!"

I *really* wish she'd stop calling me that.

"You look great," I say.

She stands. "Thanks."

The truth is she looks exactly as she did in school today, and I'm a little let down she hasn't dressed up, changed, or something. Suddenly I feel overdressed, a little too eager-looking. She turns and yells through the screen door, "I'm going out for a while, Grandma!"

"Bye, dear."

She bounces down the steps as I reach into my shirt pocket and remove the two Hershey bars, which I'm alarmed to discover have become quite soft. I hold up the sagging bars. "Would you like dark or milk chocolate?"

"Neither, thanks."

"What?"

"I'm not a chocolate fan."

Great. Now what?

She smiles. "Shall we hit the lanes?"

"I, uh, was thinking, seeing it's such a nice evening out, how about we go for a walk in the cemetery instead?"

"Oh. Well, I was really looking forward to bowling."

"It's just so noisy and smoky in there."

"I don't mind," she says. "C'mon, it'll be fun."

Hmm . . . maybe Uncle Ray isn't the expert on *all* women.

We start walking in the direction of downtown. A light breeze rustles the elms hovering above us.

"I haven't bowled since I moved here," she says. "You any good?"

"I'm okay, I guess."

"Gee, you're sure sweating a lot."

To deflect from my dampness I ask, "Which do you like better, Sting or Billy Joel?"

She looks at me funny. "Duh," she says, and throws up her hands. "Sting."

"Really? Me too."

"Why do you ask?"

"Just curious."

In the distance a train engine moans its minor chord.

"What's your favorite food?"

"Feel like I'm on a quiz show," she says. "What's with all the questions?"

"Sorry."

"Booger?"

"Yeah?"

"You okay? You seem a little wound up."

I force a grin. "Never been more relaxed. Really."

Dear Jesus . . . it's been four days since the Skin So Soft bottle. Help me! Amen.

We continue walking in silence, and I stare down at my feet. *Why did I get myself into this?*

After about a minute she says, "Your dad delivered me."

"Oh, really?"

She nods. "And your grandfather delivered my dad. Isn't that wild?"

"Just don't expect me to deliver your kids."

"You don't want to be a doctor?" she asks.

"No and no. My interests lie elsewhere." *Quick, come up with some interests.*

"Actually, I think I'd like to be a pediatrician. I love kids and I'm pretty good with science."

"I'm not sure what I want to be."

"Does your dad want you to be a doctor?"

"Definitely."

"You shouldn't be anything you don't want to be," she says. "That would be a huge mistake."

We cross Arnold Street and start south on Broadway. My hometown's main drag is devoid of cars.

"I forgot how quiet this town is," she says.

"Oh, it might seem quiet on the surface, but behind every door on this street, I guarantee the telephone lines are buzzing: 'Did you see Doc's son with that girl who used to live here? Bet they're an item.' By the time I get home, half the town will have us engaged or expecting."

"That's kinda creepy."

Does she mean she finds the idea of "us" creepy?

"That's Harker City for you," I add. "Nothing goes unnoticed, or uncommented upon."

"Tell me something," Charity says. "How do you not go out of your mind here? There's no movie theater, no bookstores, no place to buy records."

"You've lived here before."

"Yeah, but I was a fifth grader. I didn't know I wanted an interesting life."

"Well, it's not easy," I admit, "but I guess I don't miss any of those things 'cause I've never had them at my disposal."

"How do you fill your weekends?" she asks. "I'm seriously curious."

"Well, on Friday, when I return from my fencing lessons, my folks and I usually board the family Learjet.

Sometimes we fly to New York to see a serious opera, or, if my dad's feeling lucky, we'll seriously wing out to Vegas. Last weekend we went to Paris just for a serious dinner."

"Sounds serious."

"Seriously," I say, "I watch countless hours of TV, incessantly practice magic tricks, and hang out with my friend Howard."

She takes this all in, then says, "What do people say about me at school?"

"They think you're kinda . . . eccentric."

"You mean weird?"

I shrug. "Look, Harker City Junior High just isn't used to girls who dress like you and say what they think. I wouldn't take it personally. *I* like the way you dress and act."

Actually, I love it.

"Y'know, I thought things would be different when I moved back. But most of my old friends act as if I think I'm better than they are because I lived in St. Louis for three and a half years. I mean, I guess I'm not the exact same person I was back then: I'm not interested in talking for hours about what guys I find cute, I don't listen to Air Supply, and I don't particularly like to gossip, but that doesn't mean I look down on anybody."

"I'll be your friend" shoots out of my mouth—whoa!—where did that come from? "And I can't stand Air Supply."

She grins a little. "You're sweet."

Okay, so far so...good? But "you're sweet" sounds like "you're a good little boy," not "take me now!"

We are walking through our deserted downtown. Out of the blue Charity tells me that her mother has left her dad for her boss, a well-to-do St. Louis ortho-dontist.

"My dad was devastated," she says. "They'd been to-gether since high school. He really loved her. I had a feeling my mom was screwing Dr. Kilmer. I mean, how many dental hygienists work till ten on a Saturday night?"

"Is that why you moved back?"

She hesitates. "Not the big reason."

Oh, really? But I don't press.

"Do you miss your mom?"

"No, sadly. We don't get along. She always thought I sided with my dad on everything, which is completely true. But I do miss Lauren a lot."

"Lauren?"

"My best friend, the one with the twenty-year-old cat. We talk every night on the phone, and write each other daily, but it's still torture being away from her."

"Wow. That's some deep friendship."

"Yeah, it is."

For the next two blocks Charity tells me about how her grandfather died last fall of a heart attack and how now her grandmother is totally depressed. "I think our moving in with her has been good for her," she says. "She has someone to cook for and look after. She needs that right now."

I realize I'm not sweating so much anymore. The pressure of the date seems to have suddenly evaporated. Talking to Charity is like talking to Howard in a way—the conversation is effortless. Her sentences are peppered with words not commonly uttered in Dickerson County: "phenomenal," "epitomized," "vapid." I keep reminding myself about what Uncle Ray said about not allowing myself to fall into her "friend" category, about keeping it romantic. Can we be friendly *and* romantic?

After picking out our bowling balls and exchanging shoes, we settle into the far right lane. And she proceeds to kick my ass. I lob and gutter, repeatedly.

"Want some pointers?" she asks.

"Uh, okay."

With an athlete's grace, Charity demonstrates how I'm to swing my arms, place my feet, and make a follow-through motion once I've pitched the ball. Her sexy movements elevate bowling to high art. Every time she turns around to offer me another tip, my pulse speeds up—just like that first day she walked into Mrs. Crockmeister's class. I can't believe this beautiful girl is on a date with me, Mr. Toucan Nose. I especially love how when she bends down to pick up the bowling ball, she always hooks her hair behind her ear.

"Okay"—she hands me my ball—"now let's see you do it."

My game improves a little but still she totally beats me. Afterward I buy us Dr Peppers and nachos at the snack bar. I am in love.

"Where'd you learn to bowl like that?" I ask.

"My dad's a league bowler from way back, and my uncle once won three hundred bucks on *Bowling for Dollars*. So, I guess it's in my DNA."

When we saunter out of the bowling alley, I see a full moon rising in the eastern sky—a sure sign that romance is in the air? I glance at my watch: 8:17, earlier than I thought. On Broadway several high schoolers cruise in their souped-up cars. We head in the direction of her house.

"I see you're signed up to do magic for the talent show next Friday," she says. "You want to give me a sneak preview sometime?"

"The Great Linguini never reveals his secrets, no matter how beautiful and cunning the temptress might be."

"Can you do that trick where you cut someone in half?"

"Actually, I prefer quarters and thirds."

Somewhere a dog barks.

"Do you have a magician's assistant?" she asks, and I shake my head.

"Well, you do now," she says, smiling big. "I seriously want you to cut me in half at the talent show."

"You really want to be my ... assistant?"

She nods. *This is good. I see many hours of rehearsal together. I see her in fishnet tights. This is very good.*

We turn onto Arnold Street, and for the next ten minutes or so Charity tells me all about that Lauren girl, something about how talented she is as a sculptor.

"Lauren got me interested in art," she says. "We'd spend hours together at the museums in St. Louis."

I nod and try to figure out if, how, and when I should kiss her. Is a French kiss appropriate on a first date? I remember Uncle Ray saying this is a fact-finding mission, but my rapport with Charity is so great I sense I should take this to the next level tonight.

Now we are standing in front of her house. The streetlight reflects in her blue eyes as she talks on about that Lauren.

"Why don't you come in for a little while?" she says. "Meet Grandma and Dad?"

"Thanks, but I was thinking, y'know, it's so nice out maybe we should go down to Harker Park for a little while." I stare into her eyes, allowing the silence to stretch. "It's quiet there. We can be alone."

She stares at me a long moment, standing very still. "Les ..."

"Yes?"

My heart pounds—I feel a big confession coming

on. She opens her mouth a crack, takes in a deep breath, then hesitates.

"What, Charity?" My voice is a pleading whisper.

"Les . . ." She lowers her eyes and exhales.

"What, what is it?"

"I need to tell you something—"

Suddenly the front-porch lights burst on.

"Charity?"

"Yes, Grandma!"

"Who's that with you?"

"Les Eckhardt."

"Oh, hello there, Lester!"

"Hi, Mrs. Conners!"

"Why don't you two come in for some chocolate cake and milk?" her grandmother says, and opens the screen door.

"Can't we go somewhere and talk?" I whisper to Charity.

"Um, not tonight," Charity replies. "Come on in and let's just have some cake."

So close!

Seduction Tip Number 6:

Eyes Spy

The Seductive Man knows that the eyes are the first instrument in loving a woman. Go to a mirror. Study your eyes carefully. Are they bloodshot? Are your eyebrows unruly? If so, apply some strategic grooming. Now, trying not to blink too much, move your head back and forth in front of the mirror while maintaining eye contact with yourself. Every twenty seconds or so, try lifting an eyebrow in a suggestive way. Practice this for six minutes every day.

"Mo–lester, be patient," Uncle Ray advises, strumming his guitar as he sits on the edge of his bed. "Most women hate to be rushed. In the meantime try getting some experience with an easy lay."

"Huh?"

He plays a little more, then says, "I never put all my eggs in one basket. So, while this is developing with Charity, go have some fun with a slut."

"You don't understand, Uncle Ray, I am seriously in love with this girl. I want her to become my girlfriend."

"Son, you're fourteen years old! Don't ever confuse love with a need for pussy."

"That's disgusting!"

"Not necessarily. Besides, a little experience will do you a world of good. You don't want to be completely green when it comes time to fool around with this Charity, do you?"

He has a point. Why should I fumble through lovemaking—as I'm pretty sure I would—with the girl I love? Still, it doesn't feel right chasing after Regina Fallers, our school's most obvious slut.

I decide to change the topic: "When're you going to teach me to drive your car, anyway? Being able to drive will help me with girls, too, right?"

In a near whisper he says, "What do you say—once your folks're asleep—you and me sneak out tonight, huh?"

"Y'mean it?"

I watch Johnny Carson with Mom, and for the first time practically everything about the show strikes me as unbearably corny. Once I hear Mom and Dad snoring like lawn mowers, I nod to Uncle Ray, who is polishing his guitar—and dressed up sharp.

"Let's roll," I say.

Outside, the moon blooms straight overhead. I help Uncle Ray lower the top on the Corvette. As we reverse out of the drive, he switches on the radio. "If you want my body and you think I'm sexy, come on sugar let me know," goes the song.

Does Charity find me sexy? Does she want my body? Is she thinking about me right now? C'mon, Jesus, let me know.

The cool night air blows my hair and, despite it being almost midnight, I feel more awake—more alive—than ever before. Anything can happen with Uncle Ray and his Corvette convertible. Downtown, a few high schoolers are dragging Broadway. They gawk at Uncle Ray's wheels, and I sit up straighter than straight. *My first night cruising and I'm in a vintage Corvette. Not bad at all.* We glide up and down Broadway for about ten minutes listening to Rod Stewart on the radio; then Uncle Ray turns into the parking lot of Al's Liquor Store. "Be right back," he says, and hops out.

Here I am, in the middle of the night, sitting in the red glow of a liquor store's Coors beer sign while Mom and Dad think I'm safely tucked into my little bed. I've never snuck out before. I'm not too worried Mom and Dad will find out—but part of me kind of wishes they would. Just to shake them. Just to upset them. A little.

This would be worth getting grounded over. But will Jesus hold this against me?

Uncle Ray strides out holding a six-pack of Coors, which he hands to me. Soon we are thundering east out of town. The speedometer inches up to 90 mph before he slows and steers onto a gravel road. A few yards in he stops and faces me. "All right, time to trade seats."

He helps me pull the driver's seat up so I can reach the pedals. "Remember to let the clutch out slow-ly," he says as he settles into the passenger seat. "Okay, now put her in first and make this kitten purr."

I place my sweaty palms at two and ten on the steering wheel and slowly, hesitantly, lift my foot from the clutch. The car lurches forward, and the engine goes *phut!* and dies.

"Okay," he says very patiently, "let's try that again."

It takes two more whiplash-inducing lurches and engine killings, and then—I'm driving! I'm steering us down the road! 5 mph ... 10 mph ... 15 mph ...

"All right," Uncle Ray says, "take her into second." I hold my breath, say a silent prayer, push in the clutch, pull down the gearshift—and, yes! We're in second! I did it! 20 mph ... 25 mph ... 30 mph ...

As 40 mph approaches I shift into third gear—like a pro, I might add—and the fence posts in the ditch become a blur. When we hit 50 mph, I let out a "Whoooaaaa!" Uncle Ray laughs and squeezes my shoulder. I slow to make my first corner, and I'm amazed at how little effort it takes to turn the car. I'm *so* powerful!

Driving feels altogether natural to me, like a newly found extension of my own body. Uncle Ray lets me drive the back roads for the next half hour while he smokes and looks lost in thought. At one point I get this baby up to 60 mph! I want to drive all the way across the country, the planet. I feel capable of anything—anything!

"Hey, Speed Racer," he says over the wind and the whine of the engine as we near Highway 76 going into town, "let's go out to the old drive-in and celebrate, what do you say?"

I spin the wheel at the rusted Chief Drive-in marquee and turn into the long-abandoned lot. The rows of metal posts, most still sporting the gray speakers you'd hook on your car window, poke out over the weeds like periscopes. I remember seeing *Jaws* here years ago and being too scared to go into the town pool.

"Park over there by the screen." Uncle Ray points.

As we bounce over the buckled concrete, the head-lights swish across the half-collapsed white screen. I park, turn off the engine, and hand him the keys. "So, how'd I do?"

"You'll be ready for the Indy 500 in no time." He

reaches down and comes back up with two beer bottles. "Seriously, you're a helluva lot better than I was the first time."

He pops off the caps and hands me one. "A toast! To America's newest driver. Her sidewalks may never be safe again."

We clink bottles and I taste beer for the first time in my life—cold and bitter and yeasty-tasting—truly awful. *How will I finish it?* But Uncle Ray is chugging his with smooth ease and speed. God, he does everything so well. A train engine blows its lonely horn somewhere in the night. The stars shine brilliantly and abundantly over our heads. Yellow and bluish streetlamps are strung out on the town's eastern horizon like tiny Christmas tree lights. Somewhere among those lights my girl sleeps. Life has never been better.

"Y'know, I lost my virginity at this very drive-in," Uncle Ray says, staring up at the old screen. "Was the summer between my freshman and sophomore year. I even remember what was playing. *Hud*—not that we watched much of the movie." He drains more beer from the bottle and continues looking at the screen. "God, I was crazy for that girl. In some ways it never got better than it did when I was with her. Guess you could say I've been looking for her in every woman I've been with since."

"Why'd you break up?" I ask.

Looking down at his bottle, he absently starts peeling off the label with his thumb and forefinger. "We went together for a couple years. I thought it'd be forever, it was that strong. Then one night, when I was seventeen, I got into a bad fight with my old man over her.

"He found out I planned to marry her and he didn't approve, said she was some kind of gold-digging slut. Words that made me punch him in the jaw." He laughs a little, shaking his head. "He kicked my ass out of the house."

"Shit," I say, a word I'd never say around my parents. "*Was* she a gold digger?"

"Hell, no! She came from a poor family, but she didn't have a devious bone in her body. And she sure as hell wasn't a slut."

I see that half the label is off his bottle.

"After he gave me the boot, I went to her house and asked her to elope with me. She said she wanted to graduate first. Y'see, back then if a girl was married, she couldn't graduate from high school. Anyway, the thought of being in the same town as my old man for two more months was unbearable. I told her I was going out west, that I needed to get far away, but that I'd come back for her on graduation day. She said she'd wait for me and we'd get married. I hopped a freight to Texas that night. But it was almost six months before I made it back ... and by then she was engaged to someone else."

"What happened to you?"

He laughs. "What happened to me? What *didn't* happen to me! Y'see, for the first time I was out from under my old man's thumb and I went hog wild. I smoked peyote with medicine men in Taos, I shacked up with some free-lovin' hippies in Flagstaff. One morning—get this—I woke up on the Vegas strip and had no clue how I got there. A week later I was living in a microbus with two senoritas on Venice Beach."

"Sounds wild."

"It *was* wild. Anyway, when I finally made it back to Kansas, I found her at the state university. She was pissed off, of course, but I could tell she still loved me. But the thing was, she didn't trust me anymore—and no matter how hard I pleaded, she wouldn't take me back." The label is now off of the bottle. He balls it up and flicks it into the grass.

"What became of her?" I ask.

"She married a guy and they had a kid."

The train whistle moans again, this time farther away. In the north a falling star streaks across the horizon. I point and say, "Look, make a wish."

"A funny thing happened between my old man and me," Uncle Ray says, lost in his memories. "Toward the end of his life I think he came to respect me 'cause I stood up to him, 'cause I did my own thing."

"Unlike my dad," I say.

Uncle Ray looks at me, surprised.

"Your dad's a decent, hardworking man," he says. "Nothing phony about him and nothing wrong with that. Thing is, your dad and me are, well, we're just very different people."

"Dad's a total pushover."

"Maybe. But he's that way for a reason. Y'see, our old man broke his will. Roger never stood a chance. After all, he was *Roger Eckhardt Jr.* He was going to be the town doctor come hell or high water."

After a moment I say, "Uncle Ray, Dad doesn't get me at all. And he doesn't care if he gets me, either."

Uncle Ray looks at me and I explain: "It's like he doesn't even see me. He works all the time, and then when he's home, he's staring into a newspaper or fooling with his ham radios. I mean, five months ago he told me he'd build the Chinese vanishing box for my magic act and he's hardly touched it."

"Your old man, he loves you very much," says Uncle Ray. "He's just busy."

"Why are you defending him?" I snap. "You're never around. You don't know anything about what it's like to be stuck with them."

"You're right," he admits. "I don't know nothin' about that."

"Someday I'm going to run away and get a real life in a real place. And you know what? Dad won't even notice I've left."

"You really believe that?"

I nod. "I know it. He'll just go on with his ham radios and his patients and his doomsday scenarios and it'll be like I never existed."

I'm on my fifth taste of beer and feel a small headache coming on.

Uncle Ray stands and scurries off into the grass. "I gotta piss."

Another falling star in the north. Another wish?

"Shit! Jesus! Yowza!" Uncle Ray yells.

Heart pounding behind my eyes, I call out, "You all right?"

"Hurts like hell whenever I piss lately!" His back to me, he is leaning over, clearly pained. "Goddamn it, I better not have the clap again."

"What's that?" I ask.

"Never you mind, Mo–lester, just never you mind."

A *tap–tap–tap* wakes me.

The sun burns painfully through my bedroom window, and I pull the blanket over my eyes. Never again will I touch beer, I promise myself. My brain pounds like a marathoner's heart and my tongue feels like sandpaper.

There's that tapping sound again. "Les," Dad says in a soft voice.

I lower the blanket and squint. Dad stands in the doorway. "Your mother and I need to speak with you downstairs," he says, throws me a weighty look, and shuts the door. *Do they know about last night?*

I swallow four Bayer aspirins and stagger into the

kitchen, where Mom and Dad are seated like the stone-faced judges at Nuremberg.

"Have a seat," Mom says.

"We want to talk to you about your uncle Ray," Dad says in a low voice.

Uh-oh.

"Now, don't get us wrong, Ray's a great guy in many ways," Dad says. "He's got a good heart and he's a lot of fun and, no doubt about it, he's lived an exciting life...."

"But the fact remains," says Mom, "your uncle Ray hasn't exactly been a responsible person."

"He bounces around from place to place—which, in and of itself, isn't necessarily a bad thing," Dad says.

"But he's never settled down, never planned for the future. Never really grown up."

"And your mother and I fear he's a poor role model for you."

Why has it taken Uncle Ray's coming here for Dad to notice me?

"You're a smart boy," Dad says, gripping my shoulder. "As long as you take what he says with a grain of salt, you should be fine."

I roll my eyes and head back to bed.

Later that morning I phone Charity several times, but her line is always busy. Who can she be talking to for two hours? That Lauren? I have an urgent need to profess how I feel about her. I must see her now! I run to my closet, take out my black and red magician's cape and affix it to my neck, load my magic red rose inside my right shirtsleeve, and put on my black top hat. There.

"What the hell, Les?" Uncle Ray asks from the bean-bag, where he's tuning his guitar.

"I'm going to get my girl!"

"Dressed like *that*?"

Outside, I straddle my bike and speed off, my cape billowing behind me. As I roll across the Missouri Pacific railroad tracks, I pray.

Dear Jesus . . . I'll give my life to the Lutheran Church, I'll never daydream through another sermon, if You'll let her say yes. Amen.

Soon I'm on Charity's street. I ditch my bike on the lawn, leap up on the porch, and knock on the screen door. The sweet scent of cookies baking wafts out.

"Who is it?" Charity calls from somewhere inside.

"It's Les!"

"It's open!"

The living room is comfortable-looking, with lots of magazines and ceramic figurines. An old-timey organ dominates the wall behind the dining table.

"In the kitchen!" she says.

I find Charity, in jeans and a tight white T-shirt, standing at the stove, smiling over her shoulder at me. "You're just in time for cookies, Booger. What's with the outfit?"

She holds a spatula in her right hand as she trans-
fers the cookies from the baking sheet onto a cooling
rack.

"Charity, I need to tell you something." I'm breathless.

"I'm all ears." She places the empty cookie sheet and
spatula in the sink.

"Are we alone?"

She nods as she pulls off her baking mitt. "Dad's at
work and Grandma's playing a funeral."

I lower myself onto one knee, extend my arm, and
pop the rose out of my right sleeve, holding it out
for her.

"Uh, thanks," she says. "But what's all this for?"

I draw in a deep breath and remove my top hat
while slowly exhaling the words: "Charity Conners, I'm
in love with you."

She stares at me.

"There, I said it."

Wait. Wait some more. Why is she staring at me
with that *look*? Why hasn't she taken the rose? A gnaw-
ing begins in the pit of my stomach.

"Do you feel the same about me?" Ach! My voice is
a squeak.

"No, Les, I'm afraid I don't."

The rose drops from my grip.

"I'm sorry," she says. "But you see . . . I just can't. Not
like that."

When I stagger to my feet, the cape catches under
my heel and starts to rip. "But we're perfect for each

other!" I say. It is hard to breathe and speak at the same time. "I mean, we have so much in common. You said yourself I'm your only real friend in town."

"Yes, I said 'friend.'"

I swallow the knot in my throat. "But we can be so much more if you'll just give us a chance. That's all I'm asking for, a chance."

"I'm sorry, Les."

"I—I can't believe you're being so...so closed-minded about this!" I am nearly shouting, my chest is heaving. *Keep it cool—maybe she's just scared?*

"Les, what I'm about to tell you, you've got to promise not to tell a soul. Do you promise? Not a soul."

I nod.

"I like girls."

"What?"

"I'm a lesbian, Les."

"You're—you are? Seriously?"

She nods, her eyes dead serious.

"One hundred percent?" I ask.

"One hundred percent."

Feeling light-headed, I lean against the refrigerator and put my sweaty palms to my face. *This isn't happening. This isn't happening. This. Is. Not. Happening.*

"Are you okay?" she asks.

"How long have you known?" I say through my fingers.

"Pretty much my whole life."

"Have you ever dated guys?"

She shakes her head. "Guys just don't do it for me. Sorry."

"But how do you know that if you've never dated one?"

"Les, I know." She reaches into her black feathered purse, which is slung over the wooden kitchen chair, and removes a strip of small black-and-white photos, the type you take in one of those booths, and hands it to me. They show her and a very cute blonde in each picture. Their arms are around each other, and in two of the photos they are kissing. "This is my Lauren."

I hand back the photo strip and try not to look like I want to cry. "Does your mom know?"

"It's the biggest reason we don't get along. She insists I'm doing this to get back at her for something."

"And your dad?"

"It's why he moved us back here. To keep me away from Lauren."

The kitchen suddenly feels hot, cramped, and it's hard for me to catch my breath.

"No one else knows," she says. "Please don't say anything."

I nod numbly and walk toward her front door.

"Les...I hope this won't hurt our friendship," she says. "I really like hanging out with you."

I manage to ride my bike out of view of her house before the tears break.

***

Jesus . . . why? Aren't I allowed to become a man? Who's going to help me with this? What have I done to deserve this? Where is Your heart?

Seduction Tip Number 7:
That Voice

Get a tape recorder and say the following into
the microphone: "Has anyone ever told you
you have the most amazing eyes?" Now listen
to your recorded self. Are you speaking from
the deep masculine chest or the strained
virginal throat? Is your voice smooth or shaky?
Record yourself again and hone your technique
until you master the deep, alluring purr of the
Seductive Man.

I spend the rest of Saturday in bed, facing the wall,
with the covers pulled up to my chin. A lesbian in
Harker City. Who'd guess such a thing? How could I

possibly have known she was one of those? It was only a couple of years ago that I even heard the term "lesbian." And aren't they always manly women? Is this a ploy for her to appear special and different? Like her flapper costumes? *Or*—does she just need to be with the right guy? After all, she's never dated a guy. Could *I* change her? Except . . . she seems like she knows exactly who she is—and she and the blonde looked very much in love in those pictures. This is not fair. Still, if I could only convince her to give me a shot . . . who knows?

Sunday afternoon. I'm lying in bed, wondering if I will ever get over Charity, when the phone rings. Moments later Mom yells from downstairs, "Les, you're wanted on the phone—by a girl."

No. I'm not, Mom. I'm not wanted by any girl.

Still, I force myself to take the call.

"Hey, Les, it's me." Sounds like she's been crying. *Over me?*

"Hey."

"Can you meet me at the Frosty Queen in an hour?" she asks. "I need to talk to you."

Maybe she's given it some more thought and discovered she isn't as lesbian as she thought? Could she have feelings for me after all?

"Uh, okay. See you soon."

I hang up, wondering if Jesus has decided to throw me a bone. I warn myself against such feelings—but my hopes *are* up. I will play it cool. Just a sexy, experienced guy, willing to forgive her. And then . . .

When I step into the garage to fetch my bike, I freeze at the sight of my Chinese vanishing box—100 percent finished. And it's painted a fancy shiny black. A red velvet curtain hangs regally in its doorway. It looks like a million bucks.

I find Mom and Dad in the garden, on their knees weeding.

"Dad, it looks awesome!" I say. "It's totally perfect!"

Dad turns to me, shaking his head. "What're you talking about, son?"

"The vanishing box. I just know I'm going to win the talent show now."

Dad still looks baffled. "I haven't worked on it."

"Your uncle finished it last night," Mom declares as she falls back on her heels.

"Well, that was certainly nice of him," Dad says, looking almost hurt.

"I have to thank him," I say. "Where is he?"

"Hard telling," Mom says. "He drove off after lunch. By the way, young man, I thought you were sick."

"I suddenly feel better. Much, much better. See ya!"

***

The Trailways bus pulls away as I steer my bike into the Frosty Queen parking lot. I spot Uncle Ray's Corvette parked in front of one of the motel rooms. No doubt he and that Shelleby are engaging in a little afternoon delight. Stepping into the air-conditioning of the café is like diving into a swimming pool in the Sahara. Sheriff Bottoms hunches at the counter, sipping coffee. Charity gives a little wave from a window booth. As I slide in across from her, I see she has a handwritten letter in front of her, and her eyes look all puffy and bloodshot.

"Thanks for meeting me." She sniffs and tucks the letter into a stamped envelope, depositing it in her backpack.

I nod and lean back, very cool, very "sure, whatever, nothing fazes me."

Jesus . . . You can walk on water, turn water into wine, arise from the dead. So please do this one small thing for me and make Charity fall in love with me. Amen.

"I asked you here because I owe you an apology," she says.

I crinkle my eyebrows seductively. "Oh, you do?"

"I feel I wasn't entirely fair to you, that maybe I led you on." She briefly glances outside, then back to me. "Truth was, I was flattered you liked me. It felt good. But it was wrong of me and I'm sorry."

I keep waiting for the real confession: that she is, in fact, attracted to me. But what I hear is: "I should've told you from the get-go that I am the way I am. I should've been honest."

So why is *she* crying? Does she feel that sorry for me? Am I that much of a loser?

Carla, diner waitress extraordinaire, appears tableside and sets down a piece of coconut cream pie, with meringue that scrapes the clouds, in front of Charity.

"What can I get you, Les?" Carla asks.

"Nothing, thanks. Absolutely nothing."

Carla shrugs and makes her way back to the counter. Charity hands me the extra fork and says, "I got this for both of us."

I set down the fork and ask, "So why were you crying?"

"I received a Dear Jane letter from Lauren yesterday," she says, and starts to tear up a little. "It said 'There's no reason to continue our relationship,' and 'I don't want to be tied down to someone so far away,' and 'Let's stay friends.' Blah, blah, blah . . . *Blecch!*"

"Maybe, maybe this means you should be with someone . . . different. Like me."

She shakes her head. "I'm sorry, Les. It's like I said. I'm just not attracted to guys. Any guys."

God, why am I so stupid? So very, very stupid.

"Please, don't hate me," she says. "I need a friend in this place."

Her sad blue eyes. The way the sun shines through the window and illuminates her hair. I can't believe she'll never be my girlfriend. How am I supposed to just switch off who I am? From outside I hear a truck engine humming in low gear.

"Hey, I'd still like to be your magician's assistant for the talent show," she says. "If you're cool with that."

"But why would you want to hang around with me if it's not going to lead anywhere?"

"Why do you hang out with Howard?" she asks. "Is that leading anywhere?"

Outside, the engine grows louder.

"But don't lesbians hate men?"

"Where do guys get that idea? If anything, dykes and guys have a lot in common: we both love the ladies. If it helps, you can think of me as a guy with turkey tits."

"Ew." But I almost smile.

I note Sheriff Bottoms glancing over his shoulder and giving us a strange look.

"So, then," I start to ask in a low voice, "do you feel like a guy trapped in a girl's body?"

"No," she laughs. "I feel like a perfectly normal girl who is attracted to other girls."

"And you think that's normal?"

"Who gets to decide what's normal? The good

folks of Harker City? Besides, normal is overrated, and unattainable." She stabs the pie with her fork, then pops a bite into her mouth. "Mmm. You should really try this."

I taste its creamy lusciousness. *Mmm.*

"Les, I think we can be really good for each other," she says. "Y'know, be each other's confidantes. We can talk about girls we find cute."

"Might be too weird for a God-fearing, clean-living Lutheran boy like me."

"This from a guy who wears a cape and calls himself the Great Linguini?"

Now I can't help but smile. She's a sharp one, this lesbian. I clear my throat and ask, "How long have you . . . known?"

"Let's see . . . I remember being in the third grade and listening to a bunch of girls talk about boys they wanted to kiss, and I kept thinking about how I wanted to smooch Heather Adams."

"But you've never, y'know, gone all the way with a guy, right?"

She shakes her head as she chews more pie.

"So how do you *really* know you're gay if you've never done it with a guy?"

"Have you ever done it with a guy?" she asks.

"Heck, no!"

"And you know you don't want to, right?"

"Positively."

"Exactly," she says, pointing her fork. "It's about attraction, it's about who excites you, it's about... knowing."

I finally and fully believe her now. *All right, all right, all right.* I'm reluctantly convinced.

"But ...," I start to say.

"But what?"

"Never mind."

"But what?" she groans. "Just say it."

"But Reverend Bachbaugh says homosexuality is an abomination in the eyes of God."

"Is it one of the Ten Commandments?" she asks.

"Well, no."

"And wasn't Christ all about acceptance and forgiveness?" she asks. "About a year ago my mom sent me to Christian counseling in an attempt to 'straighten' me out. It was quickly clear to me that the church picks and chooses what it wants from the Bible. And they pick sin and hellfire much more than they choose Jesus's unconditional love. I don't know, Les, maybe I am some sort of sinner, but what am I supposed to do?"

"You've gotta be yourself," I say, and am proud I'm more open-minded than Reverend Bachbaugh. Still, I thank God I'm not gay.

The engine, now roaring, causes the window to vibrate. Charity glances outside and her eyes widen. "What the ...?"

A cement-mixer truck is parked beside Uncle

Ray's Corvette, its massive barrel spinning. Suddenly the large metal chute at the back of the truck pours wet concrete into the front seat!

"Holy shit!"

Shelleby's tall, broad-shouldered, bearded husband, Leo, stands beside the chute and calmly watches the concrete flow into the convertible.

By the time I make it to the parking lot, the concrete has risen to the level of the dashboard.

"Stop!" I yell, but Leo just stands there, watching the car with calm, vengeful eyes.

The door to a motel room opens, and Uncle Ray and Shelleby poke their heads out.

"What the fuck?!" Uncle Ray yells. Shelleby screams. I can see her boobs!

My uncle Ray storms outside, his arms flailing, his penis bouncing like a hot dog on a string. "You crazy son of a bitch!"

I should do something, but what?

As Uncle Ray goes to push away the spout, Leo punches him in the jaw—sending him collapsing against the car. Uncle Ray throws himself at Leo and they tussle. I run to them, yelling, "Stop it!"

Uncle Ray is no match for the massive Leo, who tucks his hands under Uncle Ray's arms, lifts him up, and drops him into the car with a splash.

Stunned, Uncle Ray is sinking fast into the gray sludge when I see Leo remove a shovel from the side of the truck.

"No!" I yell, holding out my hands as I scramble over to him.

Leo raises the shovel high. It comes down with a resounding clank. Right on top of Uncle Ray's head.

PART TWO

Seduction Tip Number 8:
Her Ears

The Seductive Man knows that a lady's ears are one of her most sensitive erogenous zones. Lobe nibbling, flicking, and sucking, along with heavy breathing and whispering, can transform any ice queen into a willing Aphrodite. When blowing in her ear, try not to use so much force as to shock her. And when kissing her ear, don't slobber or drench her. Finally, speak softly when close up. Try practicing on rubber ears commonly found in costume shops.

"Carrying on with another man's wife. It's a sin!" says Mom at breakfast the next morning. "What will people think of our family?"

Dad, unshaven, with purple bags under his eyes, just hangs his head as he stares at his coffee cup. In addition to taking care of Uncle Ray, he was up most of the night delivering twins.

"Bev, just try to keep this in perspective," Dad says. "He could've been killed."

Mom, lips pursed, sits back in her chair. "Well, Raymond is not allowed back in this house."

"Once I release him from the hospital, *my brother* will recuperate *right here*," Dad says adamantly, pointing at the table. "He's had a serious concussion. I'm going to have to observe him closely for at least a week."

Mom shakes her head. "No, not in my house he's not—"

Dad slams his fist on the table, rattling the dishes; Mom and I both flinch. "Goddamn it, he's my brother!" Dad seethes through gritted teeth. "He will always be welcome in this house! *My* house!"

Dad leaps up with such force that his chair shoots back a good three feet and slams against the wall. He stomps out.

He cursed at Mom! She looks so stunned and hurt. My first instinct is to quickly leave the kitchen so I won't have to see her cry. Instead, I go over and awkwardly pat her back while she sniffles into my shirt.

***

During second period Principal Cheavers leads the entire eighth-grade class out of school and to an idling bus. This is to be the official tour of where we are to spend the next four years, Dickerson County Consolidated High School, and we're each given a name tag (the school secretary typed "Less" on mine), so that our new principal can get to know us. When I step aboard, I see Charity sitting and laughing with Kristy Lynn Hagel, our star girls' basketball player, on the hump seat. I had no idea she and the big-boned Kristy Lynn were friends. Does Charity *like* like her? Does Kristy Lynn like Charity?

"How's your uncle?" Charity asks as I file past.

"Pretty busted up," I say, "but recuperating."

I plop down in the seat beside Howard, who's reading *Facts & Fallacies*.

"Fact—or fallacy?" he asks. "It takes longer for Newton's apple to fall to earth now than it did in 1665."

"Fact—or fallacy?" I say. "Asking annoying and pointless questions is what led to the murder of Howard Bachbaugh."

"What's eating you?" he asks, closing the book.

"I don't want to talk about it," I say, and my eyes return to Charity, who's laughing with Kristy Lynn.

"I gather Instinct cologne doesn't work so well on female *Homo sapiens*," he says.

I whirl to him and whisper, "How'd you know she was gay?"

He shakes his head. "Gay?"

"You said it doesn't work on female homosexuals. How'd you know she was?"

"I said 'Homo sapiens.' Means mankind." Then he covers his mouth. "Oh my God, she's gay?!"

"Geez! Shh! You didn't get that from me, understand?"

"That's *so* great! I mean, not for you," he says. "And that explains why she's all over Kristy Lynn."

"Is Kristy Lynn . . . ?"

"Fact—or fallacy?" Howard asks. "A girl basketball star who never dates boys, goes by the name Kris, and wears steel-toed boots to the spring dance is straight."

Does he have a point? You always hear about how there's a high percentage of lesbians in girls' sports.

I watch as Charity and Kristy Lynn laugh and flirt it up, and I feel my heart drop to the floor. Kristy Lynn is *not* good-looking, or Miss Personality. I mean, I think I'm a lot better-looking and way funnier. And, still, she's going to land my Charity. That's totally unfair. Does Charity have no taste?

Ten minutes later the bus lumbers into the high school lot.

"Look at all the cars," I say to Howard. "They must have a lot more teachers than the junior high."

"Most of those are the students', Einstein," Howard says. "Unless you're some kind of loser and take the bus, you drive to high school."

Dickerson County Consolidated High School, a one-story modern structure with massive pod-shaped concrete buildings stuck together like lily pads, resembles a sewage treatment plant, or a 1950s *Mechanix Illustrated* rendition of a moon colony. The windowless gym feels like an airplane hangar. No rope—I checked. The cafeteria looks to seat a thousand, and the library displays more books and magazines than I've ever seen in one space. Walking the fluorescent-lit curved hallways with my class, I feel spooked: how will I not get lost in this never-ending labyrinth and make it to class on time? I already miss my sunshine-filled, moldy-smelling, 1910-constructed junior high, with its high ceilings and creaky hardwood floors. I glance at Charity, who is at the back of the line beside Kristy Lynn.

An electronic buzzer blares, and the hallway flash-floods with students, most of whom look more like adults to me. So many of the girls have fantastic chests and wear jewelry and makeup, and even high heels. All the guys seem tall, and I note some of them sporting mustaches. My scrawny classmates, marooned in the current of towering upperclassmen, receive a few snickers.

Mr. Swedeson, the high school principal, a tall, thin, bald man with Woody Allen glasses, corrals us onto the gymnasium bleachers.

"All righty, people," he says, his Adam's apple bobbing up and down. "Welcome to the high school. Hope you enjoyed your tour." For the next half hour, as he speaks of how we select our own classes and make our own schedules in high school, I feel so overwhelmed I want to puke.

Dear Jesus . . . don't send me here. I'm not ready for this place. After what happened with Charity, I think You owe me. Amen.

"We'll see you all back here in August!" Principal Swedeson grins a devil's grin. "Enjoy your summer."

On the bus ride back to the junior high, no one speaks. Clearly, I'm not the only one dreading next year. And I think: Why does life have to change? Why can't things stay the same? That's all I want. For life to stay the same. Not that junior high is great, but it looks a heck of a lot more manageable than that high school.

I glance over at Charity. The way she is smiling at Kristy Lynn . . . why couldn't that smile be for me? Is my girl falling for a big-boned basketball player who wears a ponytail?

After school I am sprawled out on a picnic table in empty Harker Park, my spent eyes staring listlessly at the cottonwood trees above me as they dispense their fluffy, snowflake-like seeds into the air. As much as I want to tell Uncle Ray about Charity, I keep my promise to her. I am flailing around for something to get Charity off of my mind when I remember what Uncle Ray said about finding an "easy" girl. Should I find myself one of those? Where?

I bike down to Burger In A Box, a small, tacky fry bin by the rail yard, and rest my bike against the Tang–colored stucco siding. When I step up to the outside shelflike counter, the little window slides back and my reason for coming stares out at me: Regina Fallers.

A short girl who wears tons of makeup and has a pronounced underbite, Regina has "gone out with" at least ten guys that I've heard about. She isn't a slut per se, but she doesn't seem to have a problem taking off her bra and allowing guys to fondle her great big boobs.

"Eckhardt party of one," I quip. "My secretary made reservations for four o'clock—wait, isn't this Spago?"

Her brow draws in a confused expression. "Huh?"

"Never mind," I say. "Just making a joke."

"What do you want, Eckhardt?"

"A small vanilla cone."

As she busies herself making my soft–serve, I study her plump fanny, ripe beneath her formfitting purple uniform. Her mom, who manages Burger In A Box, is supposedly quite loose herself. I know I will never love Regina. But I am going to get me some of something.

Regina reaches through the window and hands me the cone. "Seventy–five cents."

I give her a one dollar bill and say in a husky–sexy voice, "Keep the change, sugar."

"Okay," she says unenthusiastically, and deposits the money in the register.

I lick the ice cream. "Mmm–mm. You make a killer cone, Regina."

She closes the register and stares out the window at nothing, chomping her gum.

"So, tell me," I say as I lean in the window, "how you been?"

She shrugs, still looking out the window, and pops a pink bubble. I can't resist glancing at her cleavage and thinking about fondling it.

I clear my throat. "So, Regina, I was thinking, how would you like to go out sometime?"

"Go out where?"

"How about we just go for a walk, see where it takes us."

"I don't like to walk," she says to the window.

"Well, then, we can go for a sit." I laugh a little, to help her know this was a joke.

She pops another bubble.

"Maybe we could go down to the park this evening when you get off work and hang out."

"Why?" She is now inspecting the nail on her right index finger.

"Well, I'd, uh, like to get to know you a little better."

"You've known me since kindergarten," she says between chomps.

"I think we can have a lot of fun together, just you and me."

"You mean, like a date?" she says, nibbling on a hangnail.

"Yeah, like a date."

Her cheeks puff up and her Tootsie Roll brown

eyes, shrewd beneath blue eyeliner, roam around the tiny kitchen. "You wanna take me out?"

"Uh–huh."

"But aren't you one of those gay–wads?"

"I am not!"

"But you've never gone steady with any girl and you don't play football."

"That doesn't mean I like guys."

"Yeah, well, anyway," she says, "you don't even have a car."

"But I know how to treat a lady like you, Regina." She still isn't looking at me. "So when do you get off work?"

"At seven."

"Perfect! I'll come by then."

She sighs and closes the takeout window. Mission accomplished.

"Now, Les, your uncle Ray's going to be very groggy," Dad says as he wheels into the hospital parking lot. "He's on a lot of pain medication."

The Harker City Hospital is a one–story, twelve–bed brick building on the northern edge of town, out near the high school and nursing home. Dad is the only full–time physician in a thirty–mile radius. Dr. Hayes, who is in his late seventies, works only a few days a week (and never when the fishing's good).

When we walk into his hospital room, I stop at the

sight of Uncle Ray lying in bed: head immobilized with a neck brace, bandages covering his ghoulishly bruised face, both eyes blackened and reddened, bottom lip puffed up like a poppin' fresh dinner roll. I feel my knees liquefy and everything fades to black. . . .

When the light returns, I see Dad kneeling over me with a concerned look and an old-lady nurse standing behind him.

"Les, can you hear me?" Dad asks.

"Yeah." I feel something on my right wrist and see that Dad is taking my pulse.

"You passed out, son," Dad says.

He and the nurse lady each take one of my arms and help me into a nearby chair. Uncle Ray stares at me from his bed. God, he looks awful. Will this end his womanizing ways? Is Jesus trying to teach me a lesson about the wages of sinful behavior? The nurse hands me a cup of water and I sip from it.

"Ray, how're you feeling?" Dad asks as he removes the chart from the end of the bed, flipping it open.

"I can't turn my head, my back feels like someone took a chain saw to it, I have to piss in a bottle, and I can't smoke in this goddamn hospital," Uncle Ray grouses. "That answer your moronic question?"

Dad, taking out his penlight, approaches Uncle Ray. "I need you to follow my index finger with your eyes."

Dad examines Uncle Ray's reflexes, then clicks off his penlight. "Seeing you don't have insurance, I'm going to have to release you from here, but I'll observe you at home for a while."

"I'm fine."

"Now, Ray, we don't know that yet," Dad counters. "You need to be watched carefully for at least a week."

"Where's my damn Corvette?"

Dad glances at me, as if looking for support or sympathy, then back at Uncle Ray. "The mechanic said the concrete seeped into the engine. Wrecker service is going to deliver it to the house."

Uncle Ray's eyes turn desolately out the window and he mutters, "Forgot to renew my damn car insurance last month."

I want to do something, say anything, to make him feel better, but what?

Dad nudges the food tray, where a wilting green salad and tired-looking fruit cocktail sit untouched. "Ray, be good for you to eat a little something, huh?"

Uncle Ray looks at Dad. "What'd they do with that psycho?"

"Leo's in lockup," Dad says. "The county's going to press charges."

About twenty minutes later I wheel Uncle Ray out to Dad's Dodge Charger. He gasps and winces as Dad and I ease him into the backseat. On the ride home I sit up front with Dad.

"Farmers sure need rain," Dad says rhetorically.

"Sure do," I reply. No comment on the lust for rain from the backseat.

When we pull into our driveway, there sits Uncle Ray's Corvette. Barely a foot off the ground, the front seat is filled to the dashboard with solid concrete. Uncle Ray moans as we roll past. "My poor baby."

Mom doesn't even look up from kneading her biscuit dough at the kitchen island when we help Uncle Ray into the house. Once in my room, Dad and I slowly lower Uncle Ray onto the bed. "Oh God!" he yells as his head touches the pillow. "Jesus Christ!"

"Can I get you anything?" I ask Uncle Ray.

"A buttload more of them painkillers," he says, his chest heaving.

"Not for another two hours," Dad says crisply, glancing at his watch on his way out the door.

Uncle Ray motions me over and whispers, "I need ya to pick me up some whiskey. Grab my wallet on the dresser over there and take out a twenty."

I do as he asks.

"Just go to the back door of the Dutch Lunch and knock as loud as you can," he says. "Vera should answer. Tell her you're my nephew and that I need a bottle of Jack Daniel's Black Label. You can keep five for yourself. And, kid, I need it fast."

After dinner I brush my teeth, put on a clean shirt, mousse my hair into stylishness, and slap on a little of Uncle Ray's Polo cologne. From down the hall I hear the crackle of Dad's ham radio. I inform Mom, who is knitting on the sofa and watching *Wheel of Fortune*, that I'm going over to Howard's for a little while.

"My, don't you look spiffy," she says.

"Not really."

"Well, be home by dark."

The Dutch Lunch squats on a low-end part of Main Street, next to a boarded-up pawnshop and the rail yards, and is notorious for its bar fights. It is the last place on earth I thought I'd ever go. A handful of rusty pickups and motorcycles are parked diagonally in front. I bike around to the graveled alley, look around, and tap on the weathered back door. The stench of stale beer is nauseating, and I notice several fly-swarmed trash cans overflowing with empty bottles. I knock harder, hear the clicking of the lock, the door opens, and—oh, God, why do you hate me?—there stands Brett Jenkins. I'm too stunned to run. We blink at each other for a good ten seconds. Brett seems every bit as shocked and confused as I am. Country-western music mixed with the sporadic clacking of pool balls echoes around us.

"Leth-bian?"

"I'm here to see a lady named Vera."

"Huh?"

"Brett," a gruff woman's voice calls out from behind him. "Who is it?"

A lady with penciled-on eyebrows appears behind him. Her Miller High Life T-shirt strains, and she has a trail of cigarette ash down her left boob. She rasps, "What do you want, kid?"

"Are you Vera?"

"What's it to ya?"

"I'm Ray Eckhardt's nephew."

"Brett, you know this kid?"

"Yeah," Brett mumbles. "I know the fag."

"Heard Ray's in bad shape," she says. "How's he getting along?"

"Not so hot," I say, and hand her the twenty dollar bill. "He sent me for a bottle of Jack Daniel's."

She opens the door further and motions me inside. The place is dark and thick with haze. At the end of a short hallway I can see pool tables, the jukebox, and a bar.

"Brett, y'better have him wait in our apartment while I fetch his J.D."

"Do I hafta?" he whines.

Smack! Her hand strikes upside Brett's face like lightning. I step back, terrified.

"Don't you ever give me mouth, boy!"

Brett just sighs indifferently and leads me into a depressing room. A tattered sofa faces an old black-and-white TV with tinfoiled antennas. Beside the dish-stacked kitchen table, a baby kicks in a high chair, its very wide face smeared with what looks like pureed carrots. The baby doesn't look normal: its slanted eyes are too far apart and its mouth hangs open.

"C'mon in, homo."

Standing there in that awful, smelly apartment, I know why Brett hates me. I even feel sorry for him. The dick-wad.

"Can't believe you had the gutth to come here," he says as he sits beside the baby, who is now crying and slapping its hands on the tray. "Thought you Eckhardth were too good for a playth like thith."

"Maybe you don't know me as well as you think."

"I don't wanna know you at all," he says, and grabs a small yellow plastic spoon from a glass jar on the table. Brett is feeding the baby! I am on Mars. I decide to embrace the weirdness.

"I want you to stop beating me up," I say.

"Oh yeah, and what're you gonna do if I don't?"

"I'll tell everyone at school you have a retard for a brother." I hate myself for saying it, but as Uncle Ray told me, "You gotta take no prisoners."

He glares at me a long moment, then points his finger at me. "You do that and I'll fuckin' kill—"

His mother thunders through the door and hands me a heavy paper sack and a five dollar bill. "Here ya go, kid." I place the bottle in my backpack and glance at Brett, who stares bullets at me while continuing to feed the baby.

Once outside I pedal off. The Bank of Harker City digital clock flashes 6:55. I'm right on time.

When I pull up to Burger In A Box, Regina, still in

her waitress uniform, is leaning against the building, dragging on a Kool. *Can I kiss a girl who smokes? Maybe I could, somehow, skip the kissing and just get right to her tits?*

"Hey there, Regina," I say, and brake dramatically in front of her, my back tire skidding on the concrete. "So, how about we go down to the park and hang out?"

She glances around, as if looking for someone, then shrugs.

"Great!" I exclaim. "Climb on."

I move forward on the seat as she squeezes on behind me. Never before has anyone ridden on my bike with me; it's hard to steer and even harder to pedal as we wobble all over the road. If I get a hard-on, this could be fatal.

"Finish your literature report?" I ask.

"Uh-huh."

"What book did you choose?"

"*Hollywood Wives* by Jackie Collins."

"Sounds fascinating."

About a minute later, as I struggle to steer us down Main Street, I ask, "So, what's it like working at Burger In A Box? You must see a lot of crazy stuff there, huh?"

"What's so hard in your backpack?" she asks.

"Oh, that's just a bottle of Jack Daniel's."

"Hot damn!" She squeals and squeezes me as if she had just won a new dinette set on *The Price Is Right*.

Harker Park is empty and leafy and deep with shadows—perfect for my seduction.

"Well, m'lady, let's go on over to the teeter–totter," I say as I climb off the bike.

"*After* we break out the whiskey," she counters.

With shocking swiftness she has my backpack unzipped and the bottle uncapped.

"You surprise me, Eckhardt," she says after her first swig. "Thought you were a total dweeb, but boy was I wrong."

"Hey, Les is more!"

"Heh–heh. I guess it might be."

She laughs a little and takes another swig, then offers me the bottle. It tastes like what I imagine kerosene might taste like, and it takes every ounce of self–control to swallow it. Regina is already on her fourth nip when I snatch the bottle and cap it. "Let's, um, pace ourselves, what do you say?"

The silly grin that creases her face tells me she is already buzzed. "So, you want to get down in my panties, don't you?"

"What?!" I nearly fall over.

She fires up a cigarette and says, "That's why you showed up at the Box today."

"That is absolutely not true," I protest. "You just seem like—like a nice girl. Someone I've always wanted to get to know better."

She exhales smoke out the corner of her mouth. "Guys only hit on me 'cause they think I'll put out."

I look around, all horrified, my mouth ajar, as if

looking for those dirty, dirty bastards. "I can't stand guys like that," I say. "All they think about is a girl's body. They don't care about who she is inside. So uncool."

I keep noticing she is glancing expectantly at the street.

"Trust me, Regina, sex was *the* furthest thing from my mind."

"My mom says never trust a guy who says 'trust me.'" She flicks her ashes, then inhales more smoke. "Here's the thing, Les-is-more, I'm not as easy as everyone says. But I wouldn't mind making out with you a little. You're a freak, but kinda sweet."

My heart speeds up. "Really? You mean it? About the making out?"

I'm finally going to kiss a girl! And hopefully get to touch her bazookas!

"What do you say we move to the bench over by the old cannon?" I ask, in an unfortunately high-pitched voice.

"I need some more J.D. first," she says.

"More" turns out to be about five big swigs for her, and two timid ones for me.

As we sit, I carefully place my arm across the back of the bench. She turns and looks at me expectantly. But I never asked Uncle Ray what to do once I have a girl "in position," and I haven't gotten that far in *The Seductive Man*. Sweat breaks out on my forehead and palms.

"You know, when you really compare them," I say in a quivering voice, "*The Addams Family* was a much wittier show than *The Munsters.*"

Regina looks at me as if I am singing the Soviet national anthem. "We gonna make out or what?"

"Of course," I say brightly.

She closes her eyes. My heart pounds in my ears as I stare at her glistening pink lips. *How will I know if I press them too hard? What if I am bad at this? Will she tell everyone?* Once, I overheard Stephanie Sanderson at school tell some girls about how Jared Clark kissed like a lizard. Can I somehow get out of this?

She cracks one eyelid and gives me a "what's the holdup?" look.

Time to act. A deep breath. Lean forward. I ram my lips into hers.

"Ouch!" She pulls back and rubs her mouth.

"Sorry."

"God, Eckhardt, haven't you ever done this before?"

"Of course. Yes. Definitely."

She sighs and closes her eyes again. This time I move in slowly. Wow. Her lips are surprisingly soft and moist, and her face smells of baby powder and hamburgers. I am kissing her and it is good, a turn-on. Her mouth, it opens a little bit. And my heart flutters. Now she has placed her tongue on top of mine, which lies beneath hers like a dead eel. Now what? In an attempt to cover all bases, I race my tongue around her mouth like an out-of-control power hose. I whip the sides of her mouth, and get scraped by the sharpness of her teeth.

Regina makes a choking sound, and I suddenly find myself licking air.

"What are you doing?" she asks.

"What? You—you don't care for my, um, technique?"

"Geez. Here, why don't you just sit back and let me."

Eyes closed, she ever-so-gently places her lips on mine. Feeling her soft tongue stroking mine—it is a-mazing. My skin tingles, and I fear I'm going to explode in my jeans. Me, Lester Scott Eckhardt, is French-kissing a girl! And right here in Harker Park! Not twenty feet from where Dad used to take me to ride the kiddy train! Right where I had my fifth-birthday party!

All through junior high, at school dances, Howard and I would sit by the wall and make fart noises with our armpits and jump folding chairs with the other rejects while the "studs" made out with girls on the dance floor. Now I am a stud! Legit. I will no longer gawk at couples and wonder what it feels like to make out. *I know.* Uncle Ray is a genius!

Mom will be furious if I marry the daughter of the "loose" woman who runs Burger In A Box. Well, Mom will just have to live with it. I'm not giving this up for her, or anyone.

Still kissing, I boldly drape my left arm around her shoulder and gently pull her to me. I place my right hand under her blouse and feel the soft, warm skin of her belly. Hmm ... a bit flabby but, still, what the hell, it's a girl's stomach. I slowly run my hand up until I feel the swell of her right one. Oh yes. I start to shove my fingers under the stiff fabric of the bra. *Rrrr-rrrar*—some sort of car is approaching but who cares? My digits inch around and—oh my God!—am I grazing a nipple?

Suddenly Regina jerks back and looks over my shoulder. I turn and see a banana-yellow muscle car come to an abrupt stop on the street.

"Who's—?" I start to ask, but Regina pulls me to her and places her mouth determinedly on mine. She just can't get enough.

"Reggie, you whore!"

A tall, angry guy in boots and shoulder-length hair storms out of the car.

"You know this guy?" I ask.

"Yep. He's my boyfriend."

My heart leaps into my throat. "Your boyfriend?" My first inclination is: *Must bolt!* He thunders toward us.

"Go away, Tadpole!" Regina shouts.

TAD is embroidered on his oil-stained coveralls. He's one of the mechanics at Jim's Standard Service Station. He looms over us, his Yosemite Sam mustache quivering with fury.

Meaty, greasy hands on hips, he asks, "What're you doing with this faggot?"

Why does *everyone* think I'm gay?

She points at him. "Leave me alone, Tadpole! Go back to your slut!"

Wow. Who knew monosyllabic Regina could be such a foulmouthed pit bull? I clear my throat and say in my calmest, smoothest voice, "I believe there's been a misunderstanding—"

Tadpole clinches my collar in his fist, pulls me to my feet, and shakes me. "If you touched my woman, I'll kill you."

Hard to breathe.

Dear Jesus . . . I'm sorry! Forgive me! Help me!

A panic-flash: will I end up like Uncle Ray?

"Put him down!" Regina screams, and yanks on me.

He continues to shake me violently. "You ain't never gonna tell me what to do, y'cheatin' bitch!"

"*I'm* not the cheater!" she screams. "I know what you and Rhonda did last night!"

He whirls to her and I feel his grip loosen a little. "What'd she tell you?"

"That she gave you a hand job!"

"That two-faced ho!"

So . . . so this is the real deal: I'm a mere pawn in Regina's vengeance game. She doesn't dig me any more than Charity does. Still, I was used to make another guy jealous. That's progress, right?

"Why don't I, uh, leave you two alone to discuss this . . . ," I say as he hurls me to the ground, knocking the air from my chest. White dots float in front of my eyes and the earth pitches.

"I was drunk," I hear him plead. "I don't love Rhonda. She's a whore. I love you, Reggie. You gotta believe that."

I slowly sit up and refill my lungs.

"You love me?" she says.

"'Course I do, baby," he says. "You know I do."

Aw. As the stars start to fade, and the ground stabilizes and my breathing normalizes, I watch as Regina and her Tadpole walk arm in arm to his muscle car.

"C'mon," he says as he grabs her ass. "Let's get wasted."

They pile in (he even opens the passenger door for her!) and thunder off.

My moment with Regina Fallers has passed. I am now a seasoned kisser. I've been used. But in a good way.

Seduction Tip Number 9:
The French Connection

The Seductive Man knows to keep his tongue narrow and pointed, not wide and level, when kissing. Cover your mouth with an empty shot glass. Imagining the glass is the inside of her mouth, slowly poke out your tongue as far as it will go without touching the sides. If you do touch, withdraw your tongue and start over. Make a point with the tip of your tongue and try to go beyond where you touched before. Practice this twice daily.

"I still can't believe she's a lesbo," says Howard, shaking his head.

"Keep your voice down," I snap. "God!"

We're in the locker room, in gym class, suiting up with the other guys.

Howard leans in and whispers, "Do you think if we're real nice to her, maybe buy her a hot fudge sundae or something, she'll tell us all the juicy details of her lesbian sex-capades?"

"God, that would be great. But I don't think she'll go for that, How."

"Okay. But maybe she could give us some advice on what girls look for. I mean, not only does she have experience being with girls, she is a girl. She *knows* the territory inside out."

Wearing only my jockstrap and white knee-high tube socks, I bend over to retrieve my shorts from the locker, when I feel a sudden, painful tug. What the— I've been lifted off the floor, my jock slicing into my nuts. Craphead Brett—who else?—is holding me up by the elastic band.

"Hey, look, girlth!" Brett hollers, dangling me in the air. "A piñata for cockthuckerth!"

"Put him down!" Howard shouts.

"Put me down!"

"Whatever you thay, Leth-bian."

My knees hit the wet tiled floor, hard, and it feels as if both kneecaps have shattered. Brett laughs, gives me a little kick in the side with his sneaker, then starts to walk away. Like a wobbly but determined newborn colt, I painfully pull myself to my feet and say, "My name is Les."

Brett turns and snarls, "Yeah, Leth–bian."

"No, just Les . . . Brat."

The locker room falls silent. Curling my fingers, I feel adrenaline pulsing through me, my heart pounding in my ears.

Brett strikes a pansy pose, thrusting out his hips, and says in a high–pitched voice, "Well, ya thure look like an ugly puthy–eater to me."

"And you look as retarded as your little brother."

I lunge and pop him as hard as I can in the nose. My knuckles sting like crazy. The shock barely registers on his face when I fire my left hook at his jaw, a crack that sends him staggering backward into the shower, where he slips on the soapy tiles, his feet shooting out from beneath him. *Splat!* He lands on his stupid, stupid fat butt. *My God. Did I just do that?* My hands are throbbing. I gaze down at Brett, his head hanging between his knees as he grips his nose with his grimy sausage fingers.

Why oh why didn't I do this before? Thanks, Uncle Ray. Thanks, thanks, thanks.

And then in my smoothest, manliest voice I utter, "For the last time, my name is Les."

A perfect zinger. *God, I impress me.*

I turn to face my silent, awestruck audience and give them an "and that, my friends, is how it's done" nod.

Then I hear: "Motherfucker!!!"

I whirl. Brett, all six feet one, 220 pounds of him,

rises from the shower floor like Satan's phoenix. When he charges at me, I scream like a girl and run as if my life depends on it, which it does.

Dear Jesus . . . help me! I'll never question You again. Help me, help me, help me!!

Through the gym, with Brett at my heels, I zip past Coach Turkle, who is rolling out the cart of basketballs. My socks take no traction on the rubberized floor and I nearly lose my balance.

I hear Coach blow his whistle and shout, "Get back here, you two!"

I bolt into the hallway and shoot up the stairs, taking them two at a time. Brett growls behind me like a rabid rottweiler. At the top of the stairs I throw open the door to the school auditorium and scramble down the center aisle. On stage the sixth-grade girls' glee club stands on risers doing vocal warm-ups. It isn't until they stop singing and stare at me in slack-jawed disbelief that I remember I'm naked save for my jock-strap and socks. A few girls cover their mouths. Mrs. Kohls, the music teacher, drops her baton.

One girl looks as if she's about to cry.

The sound of Brett's shoes pounding the wood floor behind me penetrates my consciousness. As I round the corner of the front row of seats, I feel his paw clutch my shoulder, but I squirm out of his grip. Soon he is chasing me down the main hallway. Mrs. Fudge, the home ec teacher, steps out of her room, and

I narrowly miss slamming into her but fail to miss the stack of papers she is carrying.

Can't run forever. Need a weapon fast. The band room. Open and deserted. I hurtle over rows of folding chairs, feverishly looking for a drumstick or trumpet. Behind me Brett is tossing the chairs out of his way as if they are made of pick-up sticks.

I grip a music stand and spin around, brandishing it like a sword in front of his face.

"You started this," I say. "You know you did. I was just defending myself."

He clutches the stand and tears it from my grip effortlessly, sending it sailing.

I snatch the closest object, a cymbal. As Brett fires his fist toward my face, I raise the cymbal—*clang!*—blocking his punch just in time. But he rips the cymbal away. Desperate, I grip a bass drum and heave it onto him—finally knocking him over. I scramble for the hallway. As I sprint past the principal's-office window, I notice Principal Cheavers looking up from his desk. He seems a bit bewildered, but I guess that's understandable.

The school's front door is fast approaching, and I try to slow down but my socks are too slick on the linoleum floor. I manage to skid into the door with my shoulder, but the release bar smacks into my hip. I am suddenly, painfully tumbling onto the sidewalk outside. Splayed on my back, I look up at the American flag whipping in the wind above me and I'm struck with an idea. I clamber to the flagpole, grab on to it, and pull myself up, clamping my feet together like a three-toed monkey! The metal is hot between my bare legs. By bending my legs and braking with my feet—just like Coach taught me on the rope—I start inch-worming myself up the pole.

Slam! The door hits the side of the building. Brett has made it outside. Damn it!

"You're dead meat, faggot!" Brett yells, looking around.

I am now right beneath the flag. I look down. At the base of the pole Brett struggles to climb up.

And from my lofty perch I see dozens of my stunned classmates craning out the windows. A second-floor window flies open and Charity sticks her head out. "Cute tush, Eckhardt!"

And then—a chorus of cheers breaks out! That's my girl! Sort of.

"Did your uncle put you up to this?!" Mom screeches as she paces the principal's office. "Where else would you learn such behavior—"

"You hit my little boy!" Brett's mother interrupts, pointing her pudgy finger at me from the chair facing Principal Cheavers's desk. "He's getting his nose x-rayed this minute because of you!" With each word her boobs jiggle beneath her Miller High Life T-shirt. Will she spill the beans about my booze run for Uncle Ray? But then she'd be admitting she sold alcohol to a minor.

"Miss Jenkins," Mom says, "let me assure you that whatever medical treatment is required, you will not receive a bill."

"That's the least you people can do," Brett's mother huffs. She stands, slinging her cracked vinyl purse over her shoulder. "You just better hope I don't sue your rich asses." She stamps out, slamming the door behind her.

Mom glares at me and I hang my head, trying to look contrite. But I'm not really worried. Mom and Dad are too busy—they never get home before six p.m.—to effectively enforce any punishment for very long.

Principal Cheavers says, "Les, this is the first and I'm sure the last time you'll do anything like this. Therefore, I'm going to leave the punishment to your folks. . . ."

"Oh, he'll be punished," Mom says. "His father and I will certainly see to that!"

"Les, why don't you go on back to class now," Mr. Cheavers says.

For the rest of the school day, whenever I pass guys in the hallway, they stop talking and stare at me in an awestruck way—are they fearing me? The girls all whisper and smile. I am a kind of celebrity. It's a little unsettling, but also more than a little fun.

Between fourth and fifth periods I'm at my locker when Darlene Kerns, a cute blond eighth grader, sidles up to me. "Hey, Les. Can't wait to see your magic act Friday night."

"Thanks, Darlene."

Is Darlene Kerns flirting with me? I'm so thrown I can't say another word.

"See you around," she says, smiling.

"Um. Yes. Right."

Wow!

At lunchtime I stride into the gym but Coach isn't there. I find him in his little office/ball-and-bat storage room, sitting at his metal desk reading *Sports Illustrated.*

"Hey, Coach, I just want to say that you were so right: rope climbing did save my life."

He looks at me, then removes his reading glasses and tosses them on his desk.

"What the hell did you think you were doing punching Brett?"

"I was defending myself," I say, stunned.

"Don't you see you've let him win," he says. "He wanted you to stoop to his level, and you did just that—"

"But I had no choice. He's always—"

"If fifteen years of teaching has taught me one thing, it's that fighting back only makes these things worse."

"So, what was I supposed to do?!" I throw up my hands. "Let him kill me?"

"First off, you should have said something to me or the other teachers."

"Oh yeah, like crying to a teacher would've helped."

"It *does* help," he says flatly.

"This is Brett Jenkins we're talking about."

He leans in, his eyes intensely focused on mine, and says very emphatically, "Have you seen Brett's jackhammer of a mother? With his home life you better believe that Brett has reserves of strength and hatred that no ordinary mortal possesses, reserves of strength and anger that are now aimed exclusively at you."

My heart stops beating. He's totally right. Brett will not let this go. He will make me hurt, and hurt bad. The question is how? And when?

After lunch I'm sitting in the library struggling to write my book report when Charity plops herself down in the seat across from mine and whispers, "I meant it. You really do have a very cute tush."

"Obviously not cute enough for you."

She rolls her eyes. "I had no idea you were such a man of action."

"I'm not really."

She picks up *The Great Gatsby*, the book I've been trying to write about. "Oh, I love this book!"

"Me too. I adore it," I say cynically.

"No, I'm serious. It's my favorite. Poor Gatsby'll do anything to make Daisy love him. What have you written so far?"

Before I can protest, she snatches my notebook and is reading it.

"It's just a very rough draft," I say.

After about a minute she says, "Booger, this doesn't sound like you read the book."

"Shh!" comes from Mrs. Armortrout, our wheelchair-bound librarian.

"Of course I didn't read it," I whisper.

"But this is a deep story about people who want to love, but can't."

"Then I already know how it ends."

"Fitzgerald, he created these very sad, very complicated characters," she continues. "They'll remind you of so many people you know. And then there's the whole death-of-the-American-dream thing. And the language it's written in—to die for."

"Okay, what do I have to do to get you to write my report? Name your price. I'll go as high as five dollars."

Charity smirks and pushes my notebook back at me. "Read the novel. I really think you'll like it. Y'know, I'm crazy about the Jazz Age."

"You dress kinda jazzy."

"It's not just the look and the music, which I admit I love, but it's the whole mentality. The flappers were really the first feminists. They weren't obsessed with marriage and babies. They drank, smoked, didn't go to church, didn't obey society's rules—they weren't defined by men. That's why my idol is Louise Brooks."

"Louise Brooks?"

"She was the best actress of the silent era—and the most outrageous. Way ahead of her time. Anyhow, read the book and tell me what you think."

"I will. By the way, you still interested in being my magician's assistant for the talent show?"

She nods vigorously. "I've already started making my costume—you'll die when you see it."

"That's it, you two!" Mrs. Armortrout says, snapping her fingers at us. "Separate right now."

Charity leans in and whispers, "Meet me at the Frosty Queen after school."

When I step into the coolness and fry smell of the Frosty, I spot Shelleby coming around the counter holding a coffeepot. And then I see her face: her right eye is blackened and swollen shut. *Geez.* Did that Leo do that?

She skids to a halt at the sight of me.

"Uh, hi," I say.

She motions me to an area by the restrooms.

"So, how's Ray doin'?" she asks in a low, shaky voice.

"He's very sore," I say. "How . . . how are you?"

She brushes off my question.

"Will you tell him I'm thinking of him?" she asks.

"Sure, of course." *Man, this is sad.*

I head over to the window table where Charity is seated and perusing the menu of songs on the 1950s tabletop jukebox.

"Let's see now," Charity says. "Which would you rather hear? Johnny Paycheck, Conway Twitty, or Boxcar Willie?"

"None of the above, thank you very much," I say as I slide in across from her.

"I swear, this town *is* frozen in time."

"Tell me something I don't know," I say.

She leans in. "So, Les, how well do you know Kristy Lynn Hagel?"

"Well, let's see. She's into basketball, and she . . . wait, is she . . . like you?"

She nods and sucks on her milk shake straw.

"I hate to break it to you, but girls like you don't exist in Harker City."

"That a fact?" she says. "You know, you'd be surprised how many girls have tendencies."

"Even if Kristy Lynn has 'tendencies,' she'll never admit it," I say. "I mean, her dad is head deacon at our church, and her mom is choir director."

"But Kristy Lynn doesn't strike me as the religious type."

"Look, Charity, I just think it's very dangerous for you to 'approach' this in any way, shape, or form."

She scoffs. "C'mon, I'm not going to shove my tongue down her throat during home ec class or any- thing. Give me a little credit here."

"I've lived in this town my whole life," I say. "If it was to get out that you put the moves on a girl, it would be disastrous for you and your family. Harker City is not St. Louis. Not by a very long shot."

"I appreciate your concern," she says, smiling re- assuringly. "And I have no intention of doing anything stupid. But Kristy Lynn, she's—"

"Your type?"

"I admit I find her very cute," she says.

"Really."

"I gather you don't."

"I don't go for the manly types," I say.

"Ha ha. You know, Les, I really admire the way you stepped up to the plate and went after me like you did. I mean, it showed real gumption. Actually, you made me realize that if there's someone I'm interested in, I have to stop thinking it to death and just go for it."

"There you are!" says a familiar voice.

I turn as Howard—what's he doing here?—strides toward us.

"Well, well, well. What an amazing coincidence. Mind if I join you?" he asks, smiling big.

Before I can protest, Howard nudges his big ass into the booth. He waves at Shelleby, calling out, "A large Dr Pepper for me! Charity, you want anything? My treat!"

"Howard," I sigh, "what do you think you're doing?"

"Any friend of yours is a friend of mine," he says, and smiles big at Charity. "Sure you don't want anything? How about a refill on that shake?"

"Howard," I sigh. Charity gives me a questioning look.

"Charity, I'm going to cut to the chase," Howard says. "Les and I need your help. We're desperate to meet girls, and, frankly, we don't know how to do it—"

"Speak for yourself!" I protest.

"I mean, let's face it," Howard continues, "all we really know about girls is what the jocks brag about in gym class, and we suspect that's mostly bullshit. You see, Charity, you can provide us with insider tips on what chicks really want in a guy."

"Howard, shut up. I'm begging you."

"Now, Les, let me hear the guy out. So, Bachbaugh," Charity says. "What's in it for me?"

Howard hands her a menu and says, "Order anything you want, as much as you want."

Howard and I watch as Charity downs a cheeseburger and fries, a chocolate milk shake, and a slice of coconut cream pie. Who knew a girl could eat so much?

"Okay," Howard finally says, rubbing his hands to-gether, "what's the secret to making women want us?"

Charity wipes her mouth with a napkin, belches a little, and says, "Here's the thing. It's got to be all about her."

"Huh?" he asks.

"I mean, be *genuinely* interested in her," she says. "I see these boys—I'm hit on by them all the time—who think they have to act like 'real tough guys.' They just don't get it. A woman wants a good, honest, caring friend."

"But I've always heard girls want excitement and fun," I say.

"We want both!" she says. "A fun and exciting friend. If you're capable of being that, you'll get some, and then some."

"Okay, I've got one—how do girls like to be kissed?" I ask.

"Take it slow and let her lead the way," she says. "Pay attention to the way she kisses you and do like she does. I like it soft and slow."

"Do girls play with themselves?" Howard asks.

"Not nearly as much as guys, I don't think."

"What about you—do you play with yourself?" he asks.

"Oh, Howard. Next question."

"Is it true that girls' boobs get hard-ons?" I ask.

"Now, that's a retarded question," Howard says.

"Kinda," Charity says, "but only our nipples harden."

"Wow."

I glance out the window and see the four o'clock Trailways bus pulling in off the highway.

"Be prepared to do a lot of listening," Charity counsels. "Girls like to talk. And if you're a guy who's willing to listen—and I mean really listen and pay attention—then you're set."

"When I asked you out," I say, "did I do all right? If, uh, circumstances were different, would you have gone for me?"

"Definitely. You seemed really sincere."

"So why doesn't Mr. Sincere ever see any action?" Howard asks.

"Oh, he will," she says. "He definitely will."

I turn away to hide my gloating grin and watch as the bus hisses to a stop and the accordion doors open.

"I have a feeling everything is going to change in high school for you guys," she says.

"Man, I hope so."

Howard, looking out the window, says, "Whoa. Wait. Well, hello there."

I turn and see HER alighting from the bus. Tall and curvy, skin the color of coffee with lots of milk, breasts pushing out of her halter top, tight blue jeans giving eloquent evidence of a perfect butt. A little dog is under her arm.

"My future has arrived on a Trailways bus," Howard quips.

"In your dreams," I laugh.

Wraparound sunglasses conceal HER eyes. Her curly black hair is pulled into a ponytail.

"A black woman in Harker City," Howard says. "Gotta be a first."

"She is hot," Charity says, shaking her head. I've never heard a girl comment on another girl like this before. *That's* hot.

Howard holds his hand to the window and makes slow, hypnotic-like gestures with his fingers, and in a low voice utters, "Come to me. Come to Howard. Look my way."

And suddenly she does!

"Shit!" I drop my face flat on the table.

Charity's giggling face is also on the table.

"It worked," Howard says—he is also one with the Formica.

When I finally have the guts to lift my face up, the woman is gone. Just then Shelleby appears at our table, holding out a bulging doggy bag with a sealed envelope stapled to it. "Les, will you please give this to You Know Who. He just loves our cheeseburgers."

I take the bag.

"Be sure he reads the note," she says pointedly.

***

After Howard pays the bill (eleven dollars, and worth every penny), the three of us head outside. Our mystery woman is nowhere to be found. Then Howard tugs on my arm and points at the little motel office, where, through the window, I see that she's exchanging cash for a room key. Her sunglasses are off and that's when—

"Holy smokes!" I say. "I know her!"

"Who is she?" Charity asks.

"You *know* her?" Howard asks.

"My uncle has, um, pictures of her."

"Is she a hooker?" asks Howard.

"I don't know. She was naked in the pictures. Really, really naked."

"Maybe she's going to set up shop at the Sleep Inn Motel here," Charity says.

"She knows my uncle. Her being here can't be a coincidence."

"But why would she check into a motel?" Howard asks. "Why not go straight to your house?"

The motel office door opens, and she emerges with the little dog. The three of us duck around the side of the restaurant. After a moment we peek out and watch her disappear into room number three (I make a mental note).

Howard turns to me and whispers, "Call me the moment your uncle tells you who she is."

"Well, y'see, I can't exactly ask him."

His eyes beg for an explanation.

"I, uh, found her pictures when I was snooping in his stuff."

Charity smiles as she straddles her bike. "Well, Booger, it looks like you've got a real mystery on your hands."

I guess I do. A *sexy* mystery.

Seduction Tip Number 10:

Your Breast Work

The Seductive Man knows that women don't like pinchers, squeezers, or biters when it comes to their breasts. Proceed at a slow, gentle pace. Never grab or be rough with her lovely orbs. Stroke the breast in a soothing manner, much like you would a Persian cat. Brush your hands and fingers softly and slowly over the nipples. If you're unsure of yourself, practice first on a grape. If the skin breaks, you're being too harsh.

Pushing open my bedroom door, I see Uncle Ray, wearing Dad's red plaid robe, propped up on pillows, staring despondently out the window. His face is more black and blue than yesterday, with shadow-like pouches under his eyes.

I hand him the hamburger bag with the envelope on it.

"What's this?" He tears open the envelope, reads the note, then balls it up and tosses it across the room.

"Whatever you do," he says through his puffy lips, "don't you let that Shelleby into this house, understand me? I want nothing to do with that needy bitch."

He points to the blue plastic jug beside the bed. "Now will you please empty my piss pot."

In the bathroom I plug my nose as I pour the pee into the toilet. When I return, Uncle Ray is snoring. I reach down, pick up the note, smooth it out, and read:

Dear Ray,

I'm so very sorry about what has happened. I love you so much. I miss you so much. I'm willing to divorce Leo to be with you. Please call me. I need to talk to you. You mean so much to me.

Yours forever,
Shelleby

Another sad, complicated Daisy. With no Gatsby to save her.

***

"Lester Eckhardt, count yourself lucky you didn't break Brett's nose," Mom huffs, then turns to Dad, who is chewing his Special K casserole. "Roger, what do you think his punishment should be?"

Dad clears his throat and says, "You know, Bev, the boy has a right to defend himself."

"Roger!" Mom gasps. "He hit someone!"

"What should he have done?" Dad takes another bite of his dinner.

The bigger question is: what's come over my mild-mannered dad?

"Think about how this will reflect on our family and the practice," Mom says. "What are we supposed to tell people?"

"How about you tell me why we are always so damned concerned about what everyone in this town thinks all the time?" Dad snaps.

Mom stares at Dad, flabbergasted. "Well," she splutters, "if you're not going to punish him, I will. First off, young man, you're grounded—"

The phone rings, shattering the exchange. I answer it before the second ring.

"Fact—or wishful thinking?" Howard asks on the other end. "The hot babe who stepped off the bus today, her bathroom window happens to be open."

"Fact?" I ask.

"Fact indeed," he says. "Ten o'clock tonight, behind room number three. Be there or be square."

I no sooner hang up the phone than it rings again.

"Hi there, Les. It's me, Shelleby. Did you give Ray the note and cheeseburger?" she asks.

"Uh, yeah."

"What'd he say?"

I turn away from my parents and say, "I don't really know."

"Oh. Well, will you please put him on the phone."

"Er—he's sleeping. Sorry. Gotta go." I hang up.

"Who was that?" Mom asks.

"A . . . friend of Uncle Ray's."

"Who?"

"Some guy named . . ." I scan the kitchen. "Stove—Stover. Ed Stover, I think he said the name was."

"Huh," Mom says.

"Uncle Ray," I say to the ceiling over the top bunk, "did you have a girlfriend in Kansas City?"

"I almost always have a chick in my life," he mumbles from the bottom bunk. "Often more than one."

"Your latest ones, what'd they look like?"

"I don't want to talk about women."

After a moment I ask, "Why'd you go with Shelleby if you knew she was married?"

"Jesus H. Christ, kid! What's with all the questions?!"

"Just curious."

"Look, I never force no one to do nothin'. It's not my problem if a chick's married."

I lean over the edge of the bed. His bruised, whiskery face is immobilized in his stained and dirty neck brace. "No offense, Uncle Ray, but it kinda is your problem now."

Uncle Ray flips me the bird before looking away.

Mom isn't snoring until almost twenty past eleven. I tiptoe past Dad's "ham shack," where he's honing in on static-filled voices from the Great Beyond, then slip out the back door, jump on my bike, and race to the motel. A light is on behind the drawn front curtains of room number three. When I slink around the motel's weed-overgrown back side, I spot Howard standing on a pile of boards, peering into a small, cracked-open, frosted-glass window.

"Scoot over," I whisper. I step onto the boards and they creak a little. The bathroom is dark, but the bed-room beyond it is lit by the flickering blue light of the TV. All I can really make out are her bare feet at the end of the bed.

"She's been lying there watching TV for over an hour," Howard whispers.

"She naked?"

"Got me."

We stand there, staring and waiting.

"You're lucky I'm even talking to you, Bachbaugh. I mean, grilling Charity like that."

"She's not *your* lesbian, Eckhardt. And it worked, didn't it?" he whispers. "She gave us both some great tips."

"That's not the point, Howard, and—"

He nudges me. My pulse quickens. Her silhouette appears in the bathroom doorway. She switches on the light, and both Howard and I lean back a little. We watch her reach in and turn on the shower. God, that belly-button ring is so—what's the word? Kinky? She's probably really wild. Stepping back, she pushes down her jeans, revealing her black silk panties, which she takes off. *Sweet Jesus!* I've never seen a real live naked woman's hoo–ha. She's furrier than in Uncle Ray's pictures. She reaches up and strips off her halter top. Boobs! Huge brown boobs! Setting foot in the shower, she closes the curtain. Her sopping wet breasts are now at our eye level, the water sluicing down her nipples. There's the smell of watermelon–scented soap mixed with steam. As she lathers her chest, I hear something: Howard's panting. And oh, wait, so am I.

The next morning, in the hallway in front of the water fountain, I pass Brett. His nose is swollen and bluish. *Did I do that?* He lasers me with his stare, and I feel ice creep up my spine. In English class Howard slips me a note: "Let's go back tonight with my dad's camera. We must immortalize her in Polaroids."

I decide not to write back.

Thank God, today is only a half day (some kind of end-of-the-year teacher conferences). Just shy of noon I'm riding my bike home, and as I start to round the corner onto our street, I hear some lady yell, "Open this door right now, you son of a bitch!"

And there she is: the Shower Lady is standing on my own front porch banging her fist on my very door. I hit the brakes. Today's short shorts are orange—with a matching tube top and shiny black cowboy boots. She's gotta be a hooker.

"You can't slip away from me, Ray Eckhardt!" she yells, pounding away, her hoop earrings swinging. "I know where your sorry ass is hiding!"

As I cautiously roll closer, she turns around, giving me the once-over. "You live here?"

I nod a little and struggle to make eye contact.

"I'm looking for Mr. Ray Eckhardt."

I stare at myself in the reflection of her big wrap-around sunglasses. It takes all my self-control to keep my eyes on her face.

"Th-there's . . . no one here by that n-n-name," I stammer lamely.

She cocks her head a little. "This is the Eckhardt residence, ain't it?"

"Uh, yes, ma'am, but there's no one here by that name."

She sighs, crosses her arms, and taps her booted foot. Above and behind her I see the curtains in my bedroom window move a little.

"You go in there and tell Mr. Nobody's Here that Cookie ain't leaving town till he comes out to the motel and talks to me. Tell him I am dug in for the duration."

"But—"

"Sonny boy, the next time you try to cover for that coward, it might help if you moved his car out of the driveway first."

As she struts across our freshly mown lawn, I can't help but linger on her legs. Man oh man.

Finding the back door locked, I retrieve the spare key Mom keeps under a ceramic bullfrog in the flower garden. Upstairs, Uncle Ray stands beside my bedroom window, peering out like a fugitive. He turns to look at me.

"You didn't tell her I was here, did you?"

"Uncle Ray, she saw your car."

"Shit!"

He hobbles over to the bed and lies down, fear showing in his bloodshot, gray-bagged eyes. Uncle Ray's hair is matted and greasy; he has almost a full beard now, flecked with gray. Big sweat rings darken the armpits of his pajamas.

"If I'm going to cover for you," I press, "the least you can do is tell me who she is."

"Just a stripper."

Wow. I settle in my swivel desk chair and lean back. "Really? I've never met a stripper before."

"There's a shock. I deejay at the club where she dances. We had a thing. Now she claims she's pregnant with my kid. Wants me to marry her."

"Is that why you came here?" I ask. "To hide from her?"

He rubs his eyes. "I told her I'm not going to marry her."

"Don't you love her?"

"What sort of question is that?"

"Well, I don't know. But what about the baby?"

He sits up and points at his chest. "Do I look like a daddy to you? Could you see me changing diapers? That's for other guys. No, sir. Ray Eckhardt has never been, never will be the settle-down kind. I'm a lone wolf, a free agent, a rolling stone. That's just who I am and I won't apologize for it. No, sir. Last thing I need is a family to tie me down. Hand me a pen, paper, and envelope."

I collect them from my desk, then watch him scribble something.

"I don't know, Uncle Ray," I say after a minute. "I think you'd be a pretty awesome dad."

He looks up at me, brow creased in confusion, as if I've just told him I think he should become a priest.

"I mean, you're a lot of fun to hang out with," I explain. "And you know a lot about people and life. And you talk to me, you know, like a real person."

He resumes scribbling, then grabs his big black

wallet from the top of the dresser. My pulse quickens when I catch sight of the wad of twenties he takes out and stuffs, along with the note, into the envelope.

"Just deliver this to her at the motel," he says as he licks and seals the envelope. "And don't lose it! There's three hundred dollars in there. I think that's a pretty decent amount, don't you?"

I nod and slip the envelope into my backpack. He hands me a ten dollar bill and winks. "And here's your gratuity, kid."

And so with three hundred and ten dollars—of hush money?—in my backpack, the most money I've ever seen, I pedal down to the motel. I've never been in the middle of an adult drama like this. It's nerve-wracking and kind of fun.

Navigating my bike across the hot, fissured asphalt of the motel parking lot, I keep wondering if I could pay this Cookie to give one of those lap dances. Would my ten be enough? Since that is her job, maybe she'd think nothing of it. I drop my bike and step onto room three's little porch. Knocking on the rust-streaked door, I can hear the applause of a TV audience from inside.

"Who is it?" she yells through the door.

"It's Les—Ray Eckhardt's nephew!"

"One sec!"

The TV goes silent, the door opens, and Cookie squints out. "Ray with you?"

I shake my head. "He, uh, wanted me to give you something."

Cookie ushers me inside, and the scent of her flowery perfume is amazing. Her dog stretches out on one of the pillows on the double bed, a small black-and-white TV rests atop a pressed-wood dresser, a lone straight-back chair lurks in the corner. Cookie shuts the door, and I see that her gleaming pink toenails match her fingernails and lipstick.

I'm shrugging off my backpack when I notice a book called *You're Going to Have a Baby!* on the nightstand, along with a banana peel. I hand her the envelope.

She opens it, eyes the money, reads the letter, then stuffs the money back into the envelope and thrusts it back at me. "Tell him I'm not getting no abortion."

I stand frozen. I have given her money for an abortion? Mom and Dad believe abortion is murder and a sin. Did Uncle Ray almost make me an accomplice to my own cousin's murder?

"You tell him I'm gonna have this baby, with or without him. . . ." And then her voice cracks, her face crinkles up, and she flings herself facedown on the bed. She's crying—no, actually, she's sobbing. What should I do? Am I supposed to hug her and say "there, there"? Will she slap me if I try? I stare at her quaking back and shoulders and try not to notice her butt too much. *Geez.* For the next few minutes I stand awkwardly and repeat the phrases I heard at my grandpa's funeral: "I'm real sorry." "You have to try to be strong." "Things have a way of working themselves out." No one has ever been less convincing.

The little dog whimpers and sniffs Cookie's face. Her chest is still heaving as she wipes her running eyes with the back of her hand. When I go into the bathroom and tear off some toilet paper, I notice a pair of purple panties and a lacey bra hanging from the shower-curtain rod. I also notice the frosted window in the shower is still open about an inch.

Back in the room, Cookie is sitting up, her back against the headboard, her knees drawn to her chest. I hand her the toilet paper.

"Thanks," she says, and blows her nose.

I shift my weight from one tennis shoe to the other. Canned laughter blares from the TV set.

"So, Ray's your uncle. You don't seem much like him." She blows her nose again. "What's your birth date?"

"February 11."

"Aquarius." She wipes the corners of her eyes. "You're kind and sensitive. Ray, he's a Cancer. I should've known better than to get involved with a Cancer. All they really care about is themselves. Why don't you sit down, sugar, you're making me nervous standing there twitchin' like that."

I settle into the little straight-back chair and watch Cookie scratch her dog under its chin.

"Man, do I want a cigarette," she says, nibbling the corner of her lower lip.

"Want me to go fetch some?" I ask.

"Thanks. Can't. On account of..." She points to her belly.

"Oh. Right."

She stretches out her legs and wiggles her toes. "How well do you know your uncle?"

I shrug. "He doesn't visit us very often."

"Has he ever talked about me?"

I shake my head.

"He's something else, let me tell ya. Leads me to think I'm the love of his life. That we're forever 'n' ever. I allow myself to fall for him—and lemme tell you, that's rare. See, I'm a dancer. You can't imagine how often I get hit on. I make it a rule not to date guys from the club, but your uncle, he just wore me down and won me over. He was the one guy I really and truly believed loved me for me, and not just for... you know, my assets. Boy, am I a damn fool!

"Thirty-two minutes after I tell him I'm pregnant, he skips town. It took me a week to track him down to this godforsaken place."

As I sit there and listen to all she's going through, I start to feel really bad about spying on her.

"Thing is," she continues, "he thinks I tricked him into getting me pregnant, but I swear it ain't true." She wipes her nose, then tosses the tissue on the night-stand. "I was on the pill when it happened." She raises

155

her right hand. "So help me God. I never meant to get knocked up, but now that I am, I want this baby more than anything in the world. And that's that."

Stealing a look at Cookie's dark-chocolate eyes, I feel my heart flutter—just like it used to with Charity. Cookie is the most exotic person I have ever met: her brown skin, the way she moves, her huge hoop earrings and hookerish clothing. What more could Uncle Ray want? Plus, she is sweet and kind and so-so-so sexy.

"Now, I realize being a father scares the bejesus out of Ray," she says. "Goes against his badass image of himself. But a kid needs a father. That's why I ain't giving up on him. Say, here I am spilling all my business and I didn't catch your name."

"It's Les."

She reaches forward and offers her hand. "Cookie."

"Cookie...?"

"Well, I'm mostly just Cookie. Like Cher is just Cher." She turns my hand over, pulls it close to her face, and studies my palm.

"What is it?" I ask.

She runs her index finger down a wrinkle that curves around the base of my thumb. "You have a long life line. You're going to live to be a very old man." She releases my hand. "Me, I'm not so lucky." She holds up her right palm and points at a crease. "See there. I'll be lucky to see fifty."

"Gee, sorry."

"That's one of the reasons I want this child now—I want something to show for my life. I'm almost twenty-three, my own midlife."

The dog leaps off the bed and waddles to the door, scratching the floor in front of it.

"Mr. Mister gotta potty," she says as she slides off the bed. She unlatches the door and walks outside.

When I step out, Cookie is sitting on the porch step watching her dog mark the grass. I settle tentatively beside her.

"Y'know," she says, "this baby would be good for Ray, too. Give him some responsibility. He's no spring chicken."

"I told him I thought he'd be a good dad."

She faces me. "What'd he say?"

"Said he wasn't the daddy type."

"Why are Cancers so goddamn stubborn? Can you tell me that?" She shakes her head. "I don't know what it is about me, but the guys I pick always end up being deadbeats and losers—God almighty, do I wanna smoke."

I can see that once Uncle Ray wins a woman over, he just doesn't want her anymore. He is one of those thrill-of-the-hunt guys. If I could have his luck with women, just once, and land someone like Cookie, I would definitely keep her forever.

Her dog is sniffing my shoes. I pat his head and say, "Think he smells my beagle."

"Y'know, Mr. Mister loves to be scratched under the chin," she says.

She is right; he waggles and wiggles in doggy ecstasy as I scratch.

"I like beagles. What's your dog's name?"

"Rusty. We're the same age."

"That's so sweet. I found Mr. Mister here shivering one snowy night at the back door of the club. Let me tell ya, it was love at first sight. I just wish the men in my life were as loyal to me as Mr. Mister. You ever been in love, Les?"

I nod, and it occurs to me that Cookie and I are in the same boat—we are both in love with people who are incapable of being in love with us.

"Love will make you do some pretty stupid shit," she says, "if you'll pardon my French."

I have a flash of myself in cape and top hat kneeling before Charity.

"I'm still a virgin" blurts out of my mouth, and I wonder where it came from.

She looks at me, a little taken aback, then says, "Well, I think that's real sweet. I think that's about the nicest thing I've heard in a long time. You stay that way until you meet the right girl, y'hear me? There's no rush, believe you me."

Not quite the answer I have been looking for.

"Me, I lost my virginity way too young," she volunteers. "And it screwed me up a little, I think."

"How old were you?"

"Fourteen."

"I'm fourteen." *And I'm ready.*

"His name was Harlan and he drove this shiny eighteen–wheeler. It was such a big, expensive-looking truck that I just figured any guy who would be driving something like that must be pretty important. Harlan wasn't much of a looker, to be honest with ya, but when I climbed in that rig I trembled at all the power he had, sitting up there on top of the world, driving all around the country, talking on his CB like Burt Reynolds. Well, I let him take my flower right then and there in his cab."

"Were you in love with him?"

"I sure thought so at the time. But looking back on it, I think it was just a way for me not to feel so lonely. Y'see, being a foster kid and all, I never felt like I belonged nowhere."

I am about to ask her what it's like being a professional dancer when she suddenly winces and grabs her abdomen.

"You okay?" I ask.

She nods. "I get this shooting pain lately. I better go in and lie down. Les, I'd really appreciate it if you'd help me persuade your uncle to step up to the plate and do right by me."

"I'll do what I can. Promise."

"Okay, then," she says as she stands. "Give him back

his three hundred dollars and tell him I'm asking pretty please for him to be a man and come out here and talk to me. Will you do that, sugar?"

"I will."

She offers her hand. "It was real nice to meet you, Les Eckhardt."

"You too, Cookie-just-Cookie."

On the bike ride home I keep thinking about how I'm going to give Uncle Ray a piece of my mind—tell him being a father isn't something he can just decide not to be, and that he shouldn't treat Cookie this way. Once I get home, I no sooner open my bedroom door than Uncle Ray, head propped up on pillows, says, "What'd she say?"

I hand him back the envelope of cash. "You're going to be a daddy."

"Jesus!" He hurls the envelope across the room. It hits my dresser mirror and bills flutter everywhere, littering the floor like green confetti. Shaken, I decide to hold off on telling him my opinions for a little while longer.

My uncle's eyes dart around crazily. He's a drowning

man searching for any life preserver. "She tricked me into getting her pregnant!"

"She said you'd say that."

"What else has she been telling you? Has she been messing with your head? Well, don't believe her."

"I just—I feel bad for her."

"You like her so much, you marry her."

"Maybe I will," I say. I've never meant anything more.

"If—and I'm saying if—I were to ever tie the knot, it wouldn't be with her. Guys don't marry chicks like Cookie."

"Why not?"

"Well, for one thing, she's a stripper, for crying out loud!"

"No offense, Uncle Ray, but you're not exactly a Boy Scout."

He reaches under his pillow, removes his flask, un-caps it, and swigs—only to throw it down. It bounces and thumps on the carpet. "Damn it! Take one of those twenties and go buy me some more J.D. And don't drink half of it this time!"

Before I can tell him off—*tap, tap, tap*. Dad pops his head in. "Hello, boys." He steps inside, asking, "How you feeling today, Ray?" and then gets all wide-eyed at the bills littering the floor.

"Er—Les," Uncle Ray says, "would you mind pick-ing up that item we discussed?"

"Little brother, you've got to try and lie still," Dad

admonishes. "With whiplash it's important you don't strain yourself. Now, let's have a look at your neck."

I snatch up a twenty and slip out of the room.

"Doris next door said she saw a colored woman yelling and pounding on our front door this after-noon," Mom says at dinner. "She also said you spoke with this woman, Les. Is that true?"

I nod as I painfully swallow a chunk of Mom's chicken-and-rice casserole, chasing it down with a ton of milk.

"Who was she?"

"Er—she was selling Bibles."

"Wasn't she cursing and pounding on our door, like Doris claims?"

I shake my head. "She seemed perfectly normal."

"But Doris said—"

"Doris Daetweiler just likes to stir up trouble," Dad barks, and sets his fork on his plate. "She should mind her own business for once."

"Well!" Mom gasps at Dad. "That wasn't very nice."

"It's the truth," Dad says. "The woman does nothing all day but look for something to gossip and gripe about."

"Doris has been a good neighbor to us through the years," Mom insists.

Dad points his finger at Mom. "She's a busybody, Bev, and you damn well know it."

"Is it necessary that you use such ugly language in our home, Roger?"

"Sometimes," Dad murmurs.

"You've been in awful spirits lately," Mom says. "Awful spirits. And I don't like it."

The doorbell chimes. Mom, Dad, and I look at one another in "who in the world could that be?" surprise. *If it's Cookie, how am I going to handle this?*

"I've got it!" I run and open the front door, and there stands Charity sporting a pair of those cat-eye sunglasses. The wind whips her red and blue bandana and flowing green skirt.

She bows and says, "Oh, Great Linguini, your devoted assistant is here to learn the divine secrets of your mysterious art."

"Oh. Sorry. I can't rehearse tonight."

"Why not?"

"Les," Mom calls out from the kitchen, "who's there?"

"Someone from school!" I yell back.

"For heaven's sake, let Howard in," Mom says. "He can join us for some strawberry shortcake."

"You, uh, wanna come in?"

"Sure you want just 'someone from school' in your house?" she asks with a smirk.

I unlatch the storm door, pushing it open for her, and she steps inside. Removing her sunglasses, she looks around. "Wow. I feel like I've walked into Beaver Cleaver's house."

I lead her into the kitchen, where Mom and Dad turn and stare in disbelief. Up till now I've never brought a girl home.

Charity breaks the stunned silence with: "Hi there."

"Well, hello," Dad says, sounding very, very delighted.

"Mom, Dad, this is Charity. Charity, meet my folks."

"Nice to meet you, Mrs. Eckhardt." Then she turns to Dad and says, "We've met before, Dr. Eckhardt."

"Oh?"

"You delivered me in an April blizzard in 1971. My parents are Dale and Elaine Conners."

Dad thinks for a moment, then nods vigorously. "Yes. Of course. I had to deliver you cesarean, if I'm not mistaken."

"Roger," admonishes Mom.

"Well, looks like I did all right." Dad beams. "How're your folks?"

"Divorced."

"I'm sorry to hear that."

"Thanks. They're fine."

Every time I steal a look at Charity, my heart still splinters painfully. If only.

"Have a seat, have a seat," Mom says as she steps around the island with the plates of strawberry-topped sponge cake.

Charity sits between Dad and me.

"You moved from St. Louis recently, didn't you?"

Mom says as she distributes the dessert. "I just received your health records from your former school. I didn't realize you and Les were . . . friends."

"Les has been so nice. I'm going to be part of his talent-show act."

"He's never given us a lick of trouble, our Lester," Dad says, reaching over and mussing my hair.

Will it be worse if I crawl under the table and die?

As we dig into our strawberry shortcake, I allow myself to fantasize that Charity is my steady girlfriend, whom my parents adore. It's so refreshing to see a pretty girl at our table. It's like our beige kitchen suddenly became colorful.

Charity says, "You know, I think I'd like to go into medicine."

"I can't recommend Kansas State's nursing program enough," Mom says. "I'm secretary of the alumni committee, you know."

"That's nice," Charity says. "But I'm interested in becoming a physician."

"Oh my," Mom says primly.

"Are you good at math and science?" Dad asks.

"She's the best," I say. "She ruins the curve in all our classes."

"I always tell Les he better keep his science and math grades up if he wants to get into medical school," Dad says.

"Hmm. I think Les is more of the artistic type," Charity counters.

Dad stares at Charity, and the painful, loaded silence stretches, and stretches, and stretches.

"Uh, delicious strawberry shortcake, Mom."

Out the corner of my eye I can see Dad staring at me.

"We've got water! Anyone want some water?" I say, just to say something.

Brring–ring! Thank God. I leap to answer the phone: the hospital for Dad.

"All right," Dad says into the receiver, "I'll be right up." He wipes his mouth with his napkin and stands. "They're bringing Lowell McIntyre in by ambulance. Sounds like a heart attack."

And he is out the door.

Mom glances at her watch. "Oh my, I'm going to be late for the school board meeting."

"Don't worry, Mom, we'll finish cleaning up."

"Hope I didn't get you in trouble over the doctor thing," Charity says as she dries a plate beside me.

I turn off the faucet. "It took guts."

"Well, anyway, your parents seem really nice. Do you always have dinner together?"

"Every night at six–thirty," I moan, and wring out the dishrag. "Come hell or high water."

"Well, I think that's great."

"You do?"

"My family hardly ever ate together," she says.

"Mom always worked late, and Dad would pick up drive-through. On the rare occasions we did eat together, it was always in front of the TV. You're really lucky."

Is this true? Am I lucky?

"So why aren't we rehearsing tonight?" Charity asks.

"I have to go see someone."

"'Someone' wouldn't be a mysterious woman named Cookie, by any chance?"

"Maybe."

"C'mon, what'd you find out about her?"

And so I tell her everything.

"Wow. Your uncle sounds like a grade-A asshole."

"Well, not really." I don't sound convincing to myself. "He's just . . . he's always been great to me."

"Yeah, 'cause you're not a woman."

"Les!" Uncle Ray calls from upstairs. "You got anything for me to eat?"

"In a sec!" I yell back.

"I have an idea," Charity whispers with a dangerous smile. "Let me take his plate to him."

"Why?"

"'Cause I have to meet this guy," she says. "Besides, it'll be fun to see his face when I walk in."

I microwave the leftovers from dinner. When I hand the plate to Charity, I say, "I'll be outside."

***

I wait on the front-porch steps. Despite the wind it's a muggy evening; the sun's an egg yolk on the western horizon. A good five minutes pass before Charity breezes out the front door.

"I thought he was going to fall out of bed when I walked through that door," she says. "He perked right up and became very flirtatious. I have to admit, he's a very charming guy. I see why some women fall for him."

"And this from a confirmed lesbian," I say as I stand.

"But I still feel sorry for the women who do fall for him. I mean, the man is clearly a misogynist."

"English, please. I've spent my whole life in Harker City, remember?"

"Means he hates women," she says as she throws her left leg over her bike seat. "See, I'm sure he claims to love women. But it's all a game for guys like him. It's about winning a woman over, then dumping her. It's all about feeding his ego."

Can't argue with that.

"Oh," she says, "he wants me to remind you to pick up his 'request.'"

Soon we're riding side by side down the street.

"So, tell me about this Cookie," she says. "Is she really a fortune-teller? Think she'd read mine?"

"You don't believe in that hocus-pocus, do you?"

"I'm not sure." She shrugs. "But I am curious. Maybe she'll tell me what to do about Kristy Lynn."

"Has anything happened between you two?"

"Last night we studied for finals in her room. We flirted a little, but I'm nervous about pushing it. I'm afraid I'll scare her off. . . . Race you!" And she tears off. I'm right behind her.

Charity beats me to the motel, and as we roll into the parking lot, I see Cookie sitting and talking on her motel stoop with Shelleby. *Gawdalmighty—when'd they hook up?*

"I see your uncle's fan club is forming," quips Charity.

Cookie waves us over. "Hey, Les!"

"Mind if I say hello?" Charity asks me.

"Might as well," I say as I climb off my bike.

"Seems Shelleby and me have a lot in common," Cookie says as we approach.

"I can't believe that bastard knocked her up and ran off," Shelleby says, shaking her head. "Y'know what? He gave me the damn clap! Why, we oughta castrate that tomcat."

"Asshole," Cookie says.

"Jerk," says Shelleby.

"Bastard," chimes in Charity.

"Good Lord," Cookie says to Charity, "what'd he do to you?"

"Nothing," I laugh. "Ladies, this is my friend Charity."

"So?" Cookie asks me. "What'd he say?"

"He just kinda blew up."

"Yeah, well, he's really gonna blow up when I sue him for child support."

Shelleby heaves herself up. "I better be getting back to work."

"We'll talk more later, honey," Cookie says.

Shelleby nods and starts for the restaurant.

Cookie looks at me. "Much as I don't want to, it's lookin' like I'm gonna have to be a single mom."

"You don't have any family who can help out?" Charity asks as she puts down her kickstand.

Cookie shakes her head. "If Ray don't come through, I'm gonna have to do it all on my own. Bambi, this girl I dance with, wasn't hired back after she gave birth 'cause management claimed she had stretch marks.

"I've saved up enough cash to see me through three months, but that's it. I don't have no job security or health insurance. They can fire me for anything, at any time. Your ass starts to sag, a few customers complain, and ya gotta hang up your G-string."

"There has to be something else you can do," I say as I sit beside her.

"There's always topless bars," she says. "But that's not really an option when you're lactating."

I suddenly have a flash vision of me in ten years as the rich and world-famous Great Linguini, a David Copperfield–like illusionist, with Cookie as my beautiful and sequined stage assistant. The whole rapt world will watch us on *The Tonight Show* as I place her inside a box and slice her into sections, then reassemble each luscious piece. Afterward, on my private jet, she and I will sip champagne and laugh about her struggling years as a stripper in li'l ol' Kansas.

"Oh, hell, maybe I should get out of the strippin' business anyway," Cookie says. "I mean, it's real hard work, dancing. My legs ache all the time. Those four-inch stilettos are murder on my tootsies. I work all night and sleep all day. But where else can a high school dropout make three hundred a night?"

"Les tells me you read fortunes," Charity says. "Maybe you can do that for a living. How much you charge?"

"You want your reading done, honey? Tell ya what, a friend of Les's doesn't have to pay. C'mon inside."

We follow Cookie inside, where she switches on the bedside lamp and places a chair beside the bed. "Go on and have a seat."

Charity sits and Cookie situates herself on the edge of the bed, their knees touching, and asks, "Ya ever had this done before?"

Charity shakes her head.

"Les, I'll need you to keep Mr. Mister quiet so I can concentrate."

I scoop up the little guy and stand in the corner by the TV, scratching him under the chin.

"Now, remember to relax and breathe slowly," Cookie says as she takes Charity's hands in hers. "I'll need complete silence for this."

Cookie closes her eyes and leans forward. After about thirty seconds she says in a somber tone, "Right away I see that you're different. You have needs that others don't. Needs that often cause you great pain. You hide these needs from most people and that troubles you a great deal."

Charity shoots me a "did you tell her about me?" look. I vigorously shake my head.

"I see there's been a major disruption in your life lately. A painful disruption. You have come a great distance." *How does she know all this?*

Cookie's voice intensifies, the words spilling out: "You are smart, a hard worker, and you care deeply about those close to you. But you're given to fits of depression. Sometimes you ruminate and feel sorry for yourself. Be careful not to dwell on the past. The past will only bring you down. . . . I see there's someone you've met recently. Someone you are attracted to. This person is attracted to you, too."

I see a grin stretch across Charity's face.

"But this person is nervous, very nervous, and frightened of what this might mean, and she'll—"

Cookie screams—startling me—and doubles over, gripping her belly.

"She'll—she'll what?" Charity asks, panicked.

I step over as Cookie falls back on the bed, curling into a fetal position.

"Can we get you something?" Charity asks.

Cookie shakes her head as she winces. "I just need to lie down."

"You want me to go get my dad?"

"No. I'll be fine. Just some water, please."

Before we leave, I slip into the bathroom, where I see two eyes—Howard's eyes—peering in the shower window. I shut the door and go to the window, whispering, "Show's over, Howard."

Before he can respond, I slam the pane down and lock it.

"You sure you didn't tell her anything about me?" Charity asks as we coast into town.

"Swear to God," I say.

"Then she is psychic. I mean, she totally nailed me."

"She pretty much did."

"Which makes me realize that I should move forward with Kristy Lynn. She only confirmed what I suspected."

"Just please be careful with that."

"Leave it to me, Booger. Now, c'mon, the Great Linguini and his beautiful assistant need to rehearse."

"It's about goddamn time you showed up." Uncle Ray's voice quivers in the darkness of my bedroom as I close the door behind me. "Now where's my J.D.?"

Seeing him lying on the bottom bunk, I remove the crumpled twenty dollar bill from my front jeans pocket and toss it at him. "Sorry. You shouldn't be drinking when you're on medication, anyway."

He grabs my wrist and pulls himself up a bit, desperation flashing in his eyes. "I need that whiskey right now, Les. I mean it. . . ."

I rip my arm free, surprised by how weak his grip is. "Don't ever grab me like that again, Uncle Ray."

"Now look, Les," Uncle Ray says in a conciliatory voice, shaking his head and smiling. "You and me, we've always had a special connection. We get each other. I ask you, who is going to take you out of this crummy town someday soon and show you the world? Your folks? I don't think so. No, Les, I am. I'm going to introduce you to chicks you couldn't imagine in your wettest dreams. You and me, we're gonna scuba dive the Great Barrier Reef. But for now, all I'm asking of you is to go get me a fifth of whiskey."

I nod. "You're so right, Uncle Ray. You've done a lot for me."

He winks and hands me back the twenty. "Thatta boy."

It's not until I'm almost to the door that I remember what Cookie said about Uncle Ray leading her to believe she was the love of his life. I stop, turn back to Uncle Ray, ball up the twenty, and hurl it at him. "Screw you!"

I spin on my heels and stamp out of the room before he gets out a word.

An hour later I'm at the kitchen table reading *The Great Gatsby*, and the book has finally taken off for me. The characters and their weird decadent world are suddenly fascinating. Whenever I read about the beautiful but fickle Daisy Buchanan, I picture Charity. *Could I end up like the doomed Jay Gatsby, dedicating my life to impressing my Daisy?*

Hearing a thumping sound in the hallway, I turn and see Uncle Ray, fully clothed, including a neck brace, stiffly shuffling through the doorway. He refuses to look my way as he passes me, muttering something about me being an ungrateful little shit. I watch him totter out the back door and into the night.

After a few minutes I pick up the phone and dial up Cookie at the motel. She answers on the third ring.

"Hello?" She sounds pained.

"Did I wake you?"

"Uh–uh." She groans a little.

"You okay?"

"Just this same damn pain."

"Listen, if you want to talk to Uncle Ray, I think you'll find him at the Dutch Lunch downtown."

"Thanks," she says. "But I'm not up to it tonight."

"I'll stop by tomorrow after school," I say.

Gatsby is telling Nick all about his early days dating Daisy, and Nick realizes that Gatsby's love for Daisy has a lot to do with the fact that she's rich. Suddenly we're all startled by a voice: "Some friend."

I turn and see Howard glaring at me through the screen of the kitchen window.

"Why'd you shut her window?" he asks.

"She's pregnant, Howard."

"So?"

"So, she's off-limits. We can't watch her like that anymore." I turn back to the book.

"Who are you? Her mother?"

"She happens to be a real nice lady," I say. "And she's going through a lot right now."

"Oh, don't even pretend you're above it," he scoffs. "I know what you're trying to do. You're trying to dump me."

"What?"

"Ever since that freak, Charity, came to town, I see less and less of you," he says, his voice thickening. "We haven't played Atari in two whole weeks."

"I'm not avoiding you, Howard."

"And next year, when we get to high school, you won't want to hang around me at all," he says. "I mean, why would a good-looking guy like you want to hang out with a porker like me? I'm social suicide. . . ."

The thing is, he's probably right. Suddenly I feel awful.

"It's just like Charity says," he continues, "it's only a matter of time before you land a girlfriend. And then I'll be stuck at home on Saturday nights watching *Twilight Zone* marathons by myself while you're out getting lucky."

"Howard, that is *so* not true."

"You're right," he says. "It's not gonna be true. You wanna know why? Because I'm not gonna be the same loser in high school that I am now. No, I'm gonna be out getting lucky, too. How, you ask? Well, you'll just have to wait and see."

And with that he disappears into the night.

I push open my bedroom door. Everything is bathed in a weird orange light. Mom and Dad, both in church clothes, stand in front of an open casket where my bunk beds normally stand. Look in the casket. There lies Uncle Ray. Dead. Still wearing his neck brace. Dad breaks down, sobbing into his hands. Mom sneers at his corpse.

"How did he die?" I ask. Mom and Dad can't hear me, I guess.

"You're finally in hell," says Mom to the body. "Where you belong."

"Uncle Ray was a good man. He was . . ."

Dad's crying. Saddest sound I have ever heard. Makes me cry, too.

Mom closes her eyes, chants, "The wages of sin is death. The wages of sin is death. The wages of sin is death."

Feel a tug at my elbow. Standing behind me: Cookie. Wearing a nurse's uniform, but with black high-heeled boots.

"Come." Gestures with her finger.

"Where are we going?"

She pulls open my closet door. Pushes away the clothes. Reveals a long, dark hallway. Follow her down it. Mesmerized by her round butt moving against her white uniform. Reach out to touch it. It shocks my hand painfully. Damn.

She glances over her shoulder, smiles. "Be very, very careful, little boy."

Hallway ends at a large red door. Cookie opens it. Suddenly we are in Charity's kitchen. Charity. Dressed in a man's gray-flannel business suit. Hair slicked back. She sets down a baking sheet of chocolate chip cookies. Says, "Hello, darling."

"Hello," say I. Start to go toward her. But Cookie steps in front of me. Brushes her hand through Charity's hair. Now they are French-kissing. Touching each other all over. Then . . .

Charity lays her cheek against Cookie's. Smirks at me. Says, "Told you so."

Charity starts laughing. Cookie, too. I hear a third person laughing. Turn and see Howard howling in the corner, where he sits holding a large container of rocky road ice cream.

I turn. Run back down the long hallway. Their laughter reverberates off the walls. The hallway seems to stretch out interminably. *Gotta get outta here, gotta get outta here, gotta get outta here.* Cover my ears, but their laughter is deafening. A door! A door! Thank God! Throw it open. Stumble into my parents' living room. The room is bathed in blue light from the TV. Mom, her back to me, sits on the sofa.

I slam the door shut, shutting off the laughter.

Mom turns to me. Her face seems to be drooping down toward her white uniform and black boots—galoshes.

"Les, come sit with me." Her voice cracker–thin in that old–lady way. "It's almost time for Johnny."

"Where's Dad?"

"Gone." She pats the cushion beside her. "Now come sit right here in your special place. The show's about to start."

On the TV Ed McMahon bellows, "Heeeere's Johnny!" and the brassy *Tonight Show* theme swells and swells.

I awake and find myself on the top bunk. It's dark outside. I lean over the side and see Uncle Ray snoring on the bottom bunk, his mouth hanging open like that of a victim in a crime–scene photo.

His flask is on the floor beside him, and on his chest lies a big maroon book. I turn my head and read HARKER CITY HIGH SCHOOL 1965 on the yearbook's spine. Why in the world would he want to look at that old thing?

Seduction Tip Number 11:

It's What's Inside

The Seductive Man knows that possessing good looks is rarely a formula for success with women. Seductiveness is a state of mind, an attitude. A good sense of humor, intelligence, and a healthy curiosity about life are traits that will make you attractive to women. Remember, if you like yourself, are thoughtful toward others, and can carry on a lively conversation, then you *are* handsome.

After school I bike out to the motel to check on Cookie. I knock on her door. Nothing. I knock louder; then I hear her faint voice: "It's open."

The air inside is heavy. On the bed Cookie is shivering on her side, her knees drawn to her chest. She wears only black panties and a white T-shirt. Her face— I didn't know black people could look so pale. Mr. Mister paws my legs.

"You okay?" I ask, instantly regretting my stupid question. I close the door.

Flinching, she shakes her head and brushes her hair from her perspiring forehead.

"Pain's worse," she gasps.

Even sick and forlorn she is beautiful.

"I'm going to get my dad," I say.

I race downtown on my bike and wrack my brain for a way that I can explain Cookie to Dad. I turn onto Broadway and pedal through the three-block business district. Dad's office is a narrow one-story flagstone building squeezed between Harkness Rexall and the senior citizen center (a prime location for a doctor). I ride around to the alley and go in the back door so as to avoid Mom, who works the front desk. Dad is in his small, paneled, windowless office, sitting behind his chart-piled desk and talking into a hand-held Dictaphone. He looks surprised to see me, pushes a button, and the machine clicks off.

"Les..."

"Dad." I am winded from the bike ride. "There's someone you need to make a house call on right now."

"Ray?"

I shake my head. "You don't know her."

"Her?"

"She's real sick. And she's pregnant. Come on!"

"Les, what's going on here?"

I tug on his shirtsleeve. "Please, Dad. Hurry."

He gets to his feet and grabs his black leather house-call bag from the bookshelf. "Go get your mother."

"I don't think we should."

He faces me. "For heaven's sake, why not?"

"It's Uncle Ray's baby. It'll only make her angrier at him."

"If I'm to examine this woman, your mother must be present."

"Then you tell her," I say. "The woman's in room three at the motel. I'll meet you there."

The last place I want to be is in the car with my parents, trying to explain why we're going to see a sick stripper in a motel room. Racing back out to the Sleep Inn, I imagine Mom's reaction to what she's about to see. My mom isn't exactly a racist, but she isn't exactly used to being around people who aren't white, either. She is mostly . . . inexperienced. Just as I turn into the motel lot, Dad's Charger pulls up beside me, and I see Mom, lips pursed, in the passenger seat.

They are stepping from the car when I climb off my bike. Ignoring Mom, I sprint past them onto the porch and knock. "Cookie, I'm, uh, here with my parents."

Cookie is still balled up on the bed, her face wincing with pain.

I wave Mom and Dad inside. Mom, the first to come in, switches on the overhead light. Cookie rolls on her back and squints.

"Mom, Dad, this is Cookie." Maybe I should say, "Not my lesbian un-girlfriend, my exotic-dancer un-girlfriend."

"I'm Dr. Eckhardt and this is my wife, Beverly." Dad sets his black bag on the nightstand. "She's a nurse."

"What seems to be the trouble?" Mom asks.

Cookie speaks of being eight weeks pregnant and of the extreme pain she is having in her abdomen. "It hurts real bad when I pee, too."

Dad seats himself on the edge of the bed while Mom wraps a blood-pressure cuff around Cookie's right arm.

"When was your last doctor visit?" Dad asks as he lifts Cookie's wrist, places two fingers over her veins, and stares at his watch.

"Three weeks ago, before the pain started."

"Is this the first time you've been pregnant?" Dad asks.

"No," Cookie says, "I had an abortion when I was seventeen."

Mom doesn't so much as blink! She just keeps puffing up the blood-pressure cuff, her eyes fixed on the little white gauge. Cookie shrieks.

Dad turns to me. "Son, you better go wait outside."

On the porch I pull the door shut and lean against the post. The window air conditioner muffles what is being said inside. Mr. Mister pads over and rubs against my right leg, and I scratch his chin the way he likes. After a few minutes I feel antsy, so I start ambling around. I spot Mrs. Stone, the ancient motel manager, staring out the office window at me. When I give a little wave, she lets the curtains drop in front of her face. Mr. Mister leads me to some evergreens around the back of the motel, where he sniffs and paws.

When Mr. Mister and I come around the front of the motel a few minutes later, Mom and Dad are helping a robe–clad Cookie into the backseat of the Charger. Mom slides into the backseat with her, and Dad closes the door after them.

"What's going on?"

"We're taking the lady to the hospital for some tests," Dad says as he walks around the front of the car. "Why don't you take her dog and put it in Rusty's pen for the time being?" Dad situates himself behind the steering wheel, and I watch as they drive off. Mr. Mister barks and whines after them. I scoop him up, petting his shaking body and reassuring him everything is going to be all right. *Isn't it?*

When I step into the kitchen at home, I'm surprised to find Uncle Ray seated at the table eating a plate of leftover Special K casserole. Crumbs cling to his beard and grimy neck brace.

"That her dog I saw you put in the pen?" he asks, cream of mushroom soup and cereal churning in his mouth.

"Cookie's sick. Seriously sick. Mom and Dad took her to the hospital."

His forehead crinkles. "What? Well, now...I..."

I shrug and walk out.

A few minutes later, in the dining room, I am setting out my American history book and study guide on the Revolutionary War when Uncle Ray hobbles through the doorway.

"Les, man, don't you see what she's doing?" he says. "This is her way of getting you all to feel sorry for her, to win you over."

"And I'm supposed to believe a drunk like you?"

He looks at me a long moment. I steel myself against the hurt I see in his eyes.

"You just, you—you used her like you use everyone," I stammer. "Like you used me. There's never going to be any Australia! You're a liar and a drunk!"

He slowly steps forward. "You want to hit me, don't you?"

"Don't tempt me."

"I am tempting you." He points at his nose, then his jaw. "Right, left, just like I taught you. Go on. Get it out of your system."

"I hate you."

"Face it, you were nothing before I came along," he

says. "I taught you how to defend yourself, I taught you how to talk to women—"

"Shut up."

"If it wasn't for me, you'd spend the rest of your life a little mama's boy. With your magic tricks and your pansy music—"

It isn't until my knuckles are stinging that I realize I have punched him. Massaging his jaw, he looks at me, surprised. "Guess it's official. I'm no longer your favorite uncle."

I run out of the room.

Mom, Dad, and I eat pork chops and applesauce in utter silence at the kitchen table. It is unnerving waiting for that moment when Mom will blow her top and read me the riot act.

Uncle Ray left the house shortly after I hit him and hasn't returned.

Earlier, when Dad came home from work, I asked him how Cookie was.

"Now, Les, you know I can't disclose patient information. But I have started her on some antibiotics. It's just a waiting game now."

It isn't until we are finishing our cherry Jell-O parfait that Mom sets down her spoon, looks at me, and says in an even, calm voice, "Tell me, Les, just exactly how did you come to know Miss Cookie?"

I draw in a deep breath and tell her the truth. Mom

nods, her face reactionless. When she finally speaks, she turns to Dad and says, "Roger, I want Ray out of here immediately."

Dad, staring down at his Jell-O, spoon in hand, sighs his patented long-suffering sigh and nods.

"The bus doesn't come to town till Saturday afternoon," Mom says. "That gives him two days to pack up and figure out where he's going. Now, are you going to tell him or am I?"

"Let me tell him," I say.

Mom and Dad exchange surprised looks.

"Please," I say. "I want to."

"Very well," Mom says. "The Saturday bus. In no uncertain terms, understand?"

I nod.

After dinner, while standing at the sink scrubbing pork-chop grease from the plates, I can smell cherry-scented tobacco wafting in through the window. Dad is seated on the front porch, smoking his pipe and reading *National Geographic*.

" 'Evening, Doc," I hear a familiar high-pitched male voice say.

I look through the curtains and see Gary Mills, the Harker City Hospital administrator, step onto our porch. A chubby man with a comb-over and no neck, Mr. Mills lives with his wife three doors to the east of us in a ranch-style.

"Why, Gary." Dad closes his magazine. "This is a surprise."

"Beautiful evening, huh, Doc?"

"Couldn't be better. Have a seat."

"Don't mind if I do." Mr. Mills settles his Santa Claus physique onto the porch swing. "Yard sure looks nice and green, Doc. Not a dandelion in sight."

"What's on your mind, Gary?"

Mr. Mills clears his throat and says in a grave tone, "I'm afraid we have a potential problem on our hands at the hospital."

"Oh?"

"You admitted a patient today, an uninsured colored woman."

"That's right."

"Who, if I'm not mistaken"—he lowers his volume considerably—"has a sexually transmitted disease."

My stomach churns at these words, and my legs suddenly feel as if they can't support me.

There is a pause before Dad says, "You read her chart?"

"You know I never look at patients' charts," he says. "Besides, I can't make heads or tails out of your handwriting."

Dad laughs, but a bit warily. "That would make two of us."

"Anyway, the director of nursing came to me this afternoon," Mr. Mills continues. "She informed me the staff is scared to go near this woman. They fear she's carrying that deadly immune virus you hear about in the news."

Panic rises in my throat. AIDS. He has to be talking about that AIDS. Certain death—the worst kind of death. But isn't it supposed to be some kind of gay disease? If Cookie has it, does Uncle Ray have it, too? Suddenly I feel light-headed.

Dear Jesus . . . don't let it be AIDS. Please.

"Why on earth would they think that?" Dad asks, and I feel a little better.

"Because the woman is a prostitute, or so folks are saying."

"This is ridiculous," Dad scoffs. "All of it."

"Doc, I can't tell you how relieved I am to hear you say that," Mr. Mills says. "Now, if you'll just have a little talk with the nurses at tomorrow morning rounds and assure them this woman isn't infected . . ."

"I didn't say she wasn't infected," Dad says, and my heart drops.

Another gaping pause; then Mr. Mills asks in a very grave tone, "You mean, she is?"

"I don't know if she is or not. We'll treat her the same as everyone else, regardless."

Mr. Mills sighs. "Doc, how many years have we worked together? Going on fifteen. Fifteen years and we've never had a dispute. Not one. And that's because we're both reasonable men who want what's best for the hospital. And for the record, I believe I've always done what's best for the patient. Now, I'm asking you to transfer her to a big-city hospital where they know how to handle a case like this."

"I won't do it, Gary. I'm sorry."

"Damn it, Roger, don't do this! The nursing staff is scared out of their wits. And who can blame 'em? We've all seen those awful images of Rock Hudson on TV...."

"I've placed her in isolation," Dad says. "And as long as the staff follows the infectious-disease precautions, which are posted at the nurses' desk and clearly direct them to use rubber gloves when handling blood and needles, there should be no problem." Dad opens his *National Geographic.* "That's all I've got to say about that. Now good evening to you, Gary."

Twenty minutes later I sneak through the back door of the hospital. The nurses' desk is vacant as I head down the hallway to the patients' rooms. I stop at a door where an ISOLATION sign hangs, check to see if anyone is around, then open the door and slip inside. Cookie is lying in bed watching TV and wearing one of those blue and white hospital gowns, an IV stuck in her right arm.

"Hi," I whisper. "Mind if I come in?"

She nods a little, eking out a smile. "Les, my little buddy."

I close the door behind me and approach her bed. She has more pinkness to her face than she did this afternoon, but darkness still rings her eyes.

"How're you feeling?" I ask as I glance at the IV tube and the plastic liquid-filled bag above it.

"Better. Your dad gave me something for the pain. You know, your folks have been real good to me. When I informed 'em I had no medical insurance, they told me not to worry, said we'd work something out. You're lucky to come from good people like them. You really are."

Second time I've heard that. "Well, thanks."

"Your dad tells me I got somethin' called pelvic inflammatory disease."

I can't help but grin—she doesn't have AIDS! *Thank You, Jesus!*

"It was a gift from your uncle," she says wryly. "Among others."

Wait, is it possible this pelvic inflammatory disease is another name for AIDS?

"Anyway, your dad started me on this IV stuff. We're gonna have to wait a few days to see if it works."

"And if it doesn't?"

"I could lose the . . ." She points to her stomach. "And possibly become infertile."

What do I say?

She grimaces and gasps as she repositions herself on the bed. "How's my big baby?"

"Out getting drunk, probably."

193

"I meant Mr. Mister."

"Oh, he's good," I say. "He gets along real well with my Rusty. I think he misses you, though."

"I miss him."

"Is there anything I can get you? Maybe something from the motel?"

She shakes her head. "Your mom brought me my things from there and checked me out. Do you know she won't let me pay her back for the motel bill?"

Mom, Mrs. Coupon-clipping Penny-pincher, paid for Uncle Ray's stripper girlfriend's motel room? Unbelievable.

"I brought you a little something." I shrug off my backpack, unzip it, and remove the Tupperware containers and napkin-wrapped silverware from inside, handing them to her.

"It's some of my mom's pork chops and applesauce."

"Bless your heart," she says.

"How're the nurses treating you?"

"You'd think I have leprosy or something, the way they wear masks and rubber gloves when they come in here. And your dad says I'm not even contagious. Shoot, this food smells good."

"Eat up!"

She nods as she cuts into the pork chop and takes a bite. I grab my backpack and dash into the little bathroom, where I don my top hat and cape.

"And now, Ladies and Gentlemen, for the moment

you've all been waiting for," I call out in a cheesy announcer's voice, "the Great Linguini!"

I sweep out and perform magic tricks for an
amused Cookie: cards, scarf and ring, the vanishing
coin. I'm about to make her fork bend when the door
opens and a gray-haired nurse, wearing a surgical
mask and rubber gloves, freezes at the sight of me.

"What're you doing in here?" she snaps as her mask
moves up and down. "Didn't you see the sign on the
door? This patient has a communicable disease...."

Cookie winks at me. "Maybe you should go, Les."

"And it's well past visiting hours," the nurse says.

"I'll stop by tomorrow, Cookie."

"Before you go," Cookie says, motioning me over.
"Please be careful."

"Be careful?"

"I have a feeling you might be in some sort of danger."

"Danger? What kind of danger?"

"I don't know," she says. "It's just a feeling I have."

When I step into the hallway, I see three nurses
huddled together whispering. Upon spotting me, they
scatter like mice.

It's almost ten o'clock and Uncle Ray still isn't home.
Rain pelts the windows. I pace my bedroom floor, rehearsing what I'm going to say to him about his having to leave here. The phone rings and I answer it.

"I kissed her!" It's Charity.

"What?!"

"Kristy Lynn Hagel and I made out tonight," she says.

"Really?" My heart sinks a little.

"We were up in my room studying for finals, and I kept dropping hints, y'know, telling her how pretty she is and stuff. She seemed to be enjoying it, so I finally said to her, 'You have very kissable-looking lips.' And she said, 'Why don't you kiss them and find out.' So I did. It was amazing."

"Tongues?" I ask, feeling my you-know-what start to harden.

"Uh-huh."

I switch off the overhead light, then move to my beanbag.

"She seemed a little nervous," she says, "but she must've liked it 'cause—get this—she's invited me to sleep over at her house tomorrow night."

"Wow," I say, breathless, as I quietly unfasten my jeans. "How, uh, far do you think you'll go tomorrow night?"

"I don't know."

"Do you think you'll, y'know, get naked with her?"

"Les, are you getting off on this?"

"No!" I'm terribly embarrassed. "That's ridiculous."

"I think you are!"

"Why would I even care what two lesbians do?"

"A lot of guys are into it...."

"I'm *so* not into sick shit like that." *Why can't I sound convincing when I lie?*

"Oh, so what I do is *sick?*"

"Maybe not sick, but it's not exactly natural," I say. "Let's face it, evolution and survival is all about reproduction, right? And if people can't reproduce, we can't survive. And two women together—they—you—can't reproduce."

"I didn't know we had an underpopulation problem." She laughs mirthlessly.

"And what do you do when you can't reproduce? You recruit."

"You've given this a lot of thought."

Actually, I'm only quoting what Reverend Bachbaugh spewed from the pulpit a few months back in a sermon entitled "Protecting Your Children from the Homosexual Agenda!"

"Let's just be honest," I say, "you're trying to pull Kristy Lynn over to your side."

"My 'side'? Les, I'm not forcing her into anything she doesn't want."

"It's like you want to destroy her life or something," I say. "It's totally selfish."

"I think you're totally jealous."

"Of a bowwow like Kristy Lynn? Ha!" I say. "You know, I feel sorry for you. I really do. It's pathetic what you're doing."

"I may or may not be a freak of nature, but at least I'm not a bigot."

"I'm sick of you! Our stupid nonfriendship is over!" I slam down the receiver and call myself every filthy word I can think of. God, I'm such an idiot.

Seduction Tip Number 12:
Size Doesn't Matter

The Seductive Man understands his penis is never too small. Penis size is not a concern for most women, who want to be pleased emotionally and intimately. The Seductive Man focuses on *her* needs by exploring her body, and not worrying about his size. He knows his hands, mouth, and brain are the real sex organs for loving that special lady.

Ten–thirty rolls around, and I contemplate going to the living room to watch *The Tonight Show* when I notice that the 1965 Harker City High Railroaders yearbook is still lying on Uncle Ray's bunk. I sit down and start to thumb through it. In the index Uncle Ray has three page numbers beside his name. On the first page is a photograph of a very young Uncle Ray, hair slicked back, standing in front of an old car and holding up some kind of auto–body–shop trophy. The following picture, his class photo, is surprisingly generic; and the last picture, in the back of the book under the heading "Unforgettable Couples of '65," features a smiling Uncle Ray with his arm around a very pretty young woman with long dark hair who is resting her head on his shoulder. I squint at the girl's face: it is my mom.

She must be about seventeen. She is wearing a big dress and is positively beaming.

Her arm is around Uncle Ray, too.

I stare at the picture for the longest time, my chest thumping. Thunder crashes.

The people in this photo look like they're much in love. I comb through the yearbook several times, but that is the only one of them together. Then, in the back of the book, on the autograph pages, I see Mom's neat cursive. "Dear Ray," it reads, "I can't tell you how much you mean to me. You have made me the happiest girl in the world. I'll love you forever. Your Bev."

Your Bev. Your Bev. Your Bev.

I have questions. I need answers. I tiptoe to the front porch, sit on the porch swing, and stare out at the rainy night. Was Mom the girl Uncle Ray told me about that night at the drive-in? Mom is nothing like Cookie or Shelleby or the other women Uncle Ray goes for. Could Mom still have feelings for him? Does she really love my dad? My parents aren't the world's most affectionate couple. But they aren't the coldest, either. They always *seem* to genuinely care for each other. But is that love? I know Mom would never cheat on or leave Dad; she's too Lutheran and too concerned about going to hell and what the neighbors would think.

Lightning illuminates the neighborhood, followed by a deafening rumble.

About an hour later headlights appear in the downpour. A hatchback with a loose muffler stops in front of our house. The passenger door opens and Uncle Ray struggles out.

"Thanks for the lift!" he calls, and tosses his cigarette.

The hatchback rattles off. I stand as Uncle Ray staggers across the lawn.

He totters onto the porch, stops at the sight of me, and slurs, "Well, well, well..."

"Er, I have something important to ask you."

"And, dear nephew, I have something important to ask you." He hiccups as he sways to and fro, rain dripping down his face. "But maybe you better go first."

I step closer to him, lowering my voice. "Did you date my mom in high school?"

"Oh boy, I gotta sit down for this." He pours himself into the nearby lawn chair. "She tell ya about that?"

"I looked in your yearbook."

From his shirt pocket he extracts a pack of Pall

Malls, tamps one out, lights it, and takes a deep, con-
templative drag.

"Was Mom the woman you told me you never
got over?"

"Ten points for the boy!" He slaps his knee, the
glowing orange tip of his cigarette floating in front
of him.

"It's too—I mean—you two don't strike me as each
other's type."

"Yeah, well, your old lady wasn't always your mom."

"Do you think that—that she still has feelings for
you?"

He guffaws. "Homicidal feelings. And even if she
still felt something good for me, she'd never act on it.
Or admit it."

"Why do you think she took up with Dad?"

He shrugs. "After someone like me she probably
wanted stability. And if there was anyone who could
provide that it was Roger Eckhardt Jr."

"So she *settled* for my dad?"

He shakes his head. "I think she really loves him."

"You're just saying that."

"No, your old man's good to her, and she loves
him for it. . . . It's my turn to ask you for something."
He reaches into his jacket and produces a handgun,
the one I found in his duffel bag. *Is this the danger
Cookie had a feeling about?* He holds the gun barrel in
his right hand and points the butt at me. "I want you
to kill me."

"Shut up, Uncle Ray."

"I mean it, goddamn it!" He continues to hold it out to me. "You know you want to. Y'said you hated me. I'm giving you permission."

"You're just drunk."

"Yeah, and what do I have to live for? Huh? Tell me! We both know I'm never gonna succeed at anything, that I'm gonna keep on hurting people. You're the only person who ever respected me, and now I've lost that—"

"Uncle Ray, stop it. . . ."

"You're a minor." He thrusts the gun at me again, but I step back. "You shoot me and you won't even go to jail. Just tell the judge I shot at you first. Look, do it for Cookie and all the other countless women whose lives I've destroyed. Hell, do it for the whole goddamn female gender."

I roll my eyes and have started for the house when I hear the click of the hammer.

Uncle Ray has the barrel pressed against his temple. My heart stops.

"This might be the one thing in my life I do right," he says.

"You wanna do something right for once in your life? Don't make your only brother have to find your brains splattered all over the front porch."

"He's seen a hundred dead bodies—"

"But never his brother's. It would kill him. You know it would."

Ka-boom!

I flinch, but it's thunder. *Thank You, Jesus!* I breathe again.

Uncle Ray looks at me for a long moment, then lowers the gun. "You're right," he mumbles. "It would kill him."

He hangs his head, dropping the gun into his lap. I reach down and snatch it from him. He doesn't even look up at me.

"C'mon," I say, "let's try and get some sleep. Been a long day."

"Gonna get longer."

It may at that.

Seduction Tip Number 13:

All of Her

The truly Seductive Man never views a woman as a conquest, with each sexual success being an ego builder, or a way to gain the admiration of other men. He genuinely likes the woman he's with: he listens to her, he communicates with her, he's patient with her, he cares about her needs and happiness. The Seductive Man knows that great sex is possible only when he takes the time and interest to fully know and appreciate her.

"It true your uncle's black girlfriend has AIDS?"

I stop chewing my cabbage biscuit and glare at

Kenny Stone, a dumb seventh grader, over the lunch-room table.

"Y'know," he continues, "my aunt who runs the motel had to throw away the sheets from that woman's room and scrub down the mattress with ammonia so her next customer wouldn't get it."

"Kenny," I say, clearing my throat, "your aunt is an idiot. I'm guessing it runs in the family."

Tray in hand, I stand and look for another place to sit. Charity is across from Kristy Lynn. Howard, who is not speaking to me, is at the geek table. *God, what's wrong with me? Why don't I have more friends?*

I head for the gym to climb some rope.

After school I see Charity about to straddle her bike and I run over. "Charity, can we talk?"

She looks at me, still clearly pissed off.

"I'm sorry about what I said last night on the phone," I say. "It was insensitive of me. And you're so right, I am a little jealous of Kristy Lynn."

"Oh, Booger." She throws her arms around my neck and squeezes me.

"So, are we still on for the talent show tonight?" I ask.

"I'm game, if you are."

I pull my bike from the stand.

"Where you headed?" she asks.

"To see Cookie at the hospital."

"Mind if I join you?"

"I'd like that."

Soon we're coasting down the Walnut Street hill, the steepest hill in town.

"Maybe we should rehearse one more time before tonight," she says. "Iron out the kinks."

"Probably not a bad idea."

We gain momentum, and as the Broadway intersection approaches, I clinch the brakes only to discover—they are gone! Panic catches in my throat and I know instantly what has happened. I go to stick out my feet but the speed is too great, the incline too steep.

"Les!" Charity yells. "Stop!"

"Brett cut my brakes!" I shriek.

I shoot through the intersection and narrowly miss the grille of an oncoming UPS truck. Up ahead, less than a block away, a slow-moving freight train dead-ends the street.

"Les!"

I am downtown, which means no green lawns, no cushioned landings in sight. As I veer to the right, my front tire strikes the curb, catapulting me like a cowboy from a bucking bronco. And in that moment, as I am airborne, time slows, just like they say it does. I look down at the approaching concrete facade of Burger In A Box and anticipate how painful my crash will be, and how I shouldn't let my brain get smushed.

Wham!

The right side of my body hits the sidewalk, and I

feel as if I have been struck by that truck. After a million little particles of light explode in front of my eyes, my arm begins to burn, and now I feel shaky all over, and nauseous. *Mom. I want my mom.* When the lights fade and the world comes into focus, I see my right arm covered in blood and Charity standing over me, fear contorting her face.

"Oh my God, Les!"

"How's my bike?"

She helps me up—the ground feels as if it is pitching. Regina rushes out of the diner and shows Charity and me into the little bathroom behind the fry bin. Even hands me a fresh bar of Irish Spring.

"Go on and clean yourself right up," Charity orders, turning on the faucet. "I'll call your folks."

I stare at myself in the mirror: I am ultrawhite and my chin is scraped and raw. Feeling as if I might throw up, I sit on the toilet and cradle my pounding head in my hands.

"Your mom's on her way," Charity says, and goes about dampening paper towels.

Within ten minutes Mom rushes in in her crisp white uniform, carrying a gleaming first-aid kit, massive concern written all over her face.

"You're going to need stitches," she says in full Super Nurse mode as she dabs alcohol-soaked cotton balls on my wounds. "How did this happen?"

"Lost control of my bike."

Mom takes excellent care of me.

"Mom," I say as she pours iodine onto my knee gash. "I love you."

"Well, gee, honey. You're not dying—and I love you, too."

Later, at Dad's office, Charity observes as Dad sews four stitches into my arm and disinfects and dresses my other wounds. According to the X-rays, I didn't break anything, but I have sprained my arm and have to wear a sling.

"But I need my right arm for the talent show to-night," I tell Dad.

"Nope, young man, there'll be no talent show for you tonight," Mom says.

"Aw, Mom, c'mon."

"You're in no condition to perform," she insists.

Charity steps up and says, "I'm his assistant, Mrs. Eckhardt. I can help him. I promise you we'll be careful."

"Yeah, Mom," I say pleadingly. "I'll be assisted."

"Well, all right," Mom says. "Come now, I'll drive you home."

In our driveway Mom unloads my bike from her trunk.

"I have to get back to work, honey," Mom says as she shuts the trunk. "Try to get some rest. I'll be home at six sharp." She climbs in her Buick and is off.

I crouch down and examine my bike's damage: the front tire spokes are bent, as is the front fender, and the handlebars look out of whack. Then I notice something strange out of the corner of my eye: an unfamiliar blue Ford pickup parked across the street. An angry, redneck-looking guy sits in the cab, watching me, a shotgun rack hanging behind him. The driver's door opens, and I quickly turn back to my bike, debating whether to run or not. I listen as heavy footfalls approach.

"Hey, you! Boy!"

I look up. Leo, Shelleby's husband, hulks over me, his Paul Bunyan–like frame eclipsing the sun.

"Your goddamn uncle gave my wife the clap!"

"Er—sorry."

"You tell that sorry son of a bitch that I'm outta jail and he can't hide in your house forever. You tell him we got us a score to settle."

He spins on his concrete–encrusted cowboy boots and swaggers back to his truck. What exactly is this clap?

As expected, I find the back door of our house locked. Then I notice someone leaning against our backyard fence—a large brown–bearded guy in a dirty T-shirt; he has to be Leo's brother. With trembling hands I slip the key out from beneath the ceramic bullfrog and thrust it into the lock. Once inside, I bolt the door and exhale.

Upstairs I find my bedroom door locked and jiggle the handle. "Uncle Ray, it's me."

"You alone?"

"Uh–huh."

The door cracks; Uncle Ray, looking haggard, peers out, then opens the door all the way. "What happened to you?" he asks, relocking the door behind me.

"The outcome of your swell advice on standing up to Brett."

The curtains are drawn, and Uncle Ray is in desperate need of some deodorant.

"You didn't tell the Neanderthal Brothers I was here, did you?" he asks.

" 'Course not."

"Story is, you haven't seen me, you have no idea where I am. Understand?"

"Uncle Ray, how many more people are going to show up here looking for you?"

He hobbles to the window and carefully peeks out. "He and his fellow mouth–breathers have been out there all afternoon."

"Why don't you call the police?"

He shakes his head and lets the curtain fall back into place. "Hey, where'd you put my gun? Can't find it anywhere."

"I threw it in old man Krause's pond."

Stricken, he faces me. He winces and smites his forehead with his right palm. "You didn't. Please tell me you didn't."

"I was afraid you were going to kill yourself!" I say.

"Does your old man have a gun?"

"This is Dad we're talking about."

He rubs his temples. "Listen up," he says. "When it gets dark tonight, you're gonna help me get into the trunk of your dad's car, while it's still parked in the garage. Then you're gonna drive me down to the rail yards, and I'm gonna hop a freight out of this bad-luck burg."

"Uncle Ray, I've driven exactly once in my life! Besides, those guys will just follow us."

He nods, looks down at the floor, and resumes rubbing his temples.

"Plus," I say, "I have my talent show tonight."

"Your show! This is my life we're talking about here! Hold on, I've got it! Saw it in an old gangster movie: late tonight you'll go outside dressed like me, right? You start walking away down the street and they chase you down, thinking you're me. Meanwhile, I climb in their car and drive off."

"And I'm left to face them? I don't think so."

Uncle Ray bites the corner of his lips, continues rubbing his temples.

"Maybe Dad'll have an idea," I volunteer.

"No," Uncle Ray says. "We're not involving him in this. Absolutely not! This is our problem."

"Don't you mean your problem?"

He collapses in my desk chair and buries his face in his arms. "I'm so screwed."

As I look around, I see my magician's cape and hat on the dresser, and the idea strikes me like an epiphany. "I've got it," I say. "I know how we can get you out of here."

He raises his head, looking at me. "What? Tell me! Talk to me!"

"I promise I'll get you on a train tonight on one condition."

"What?"

"You have to call Cookie, talk to her, and tell her goodbye."

He shakes his head. "I'm not good with shit like that."

"If you can sweet-talk her into falling in love with you, the least you can do is give her a decent goodbye. Do it or I won't help you."

"Shit. Jesus H. Christ. Damn it. Oh, all right."

"Roger, did you notice there's two men in a pickup parked across the street?" Mom says that evening at the dinner table. "They seem to be watching our house."

Dad, chewing his Shake 'n Bake chicken, leans forward in his chair, pushes back the curtains, and squints out the window. "You don't say."

I exchange worried glances with Uncle Ray, who is seated across the table from me. I clear my throat and say, "Uncle Ray is going to go with us to the talent show tonight."

"That's great," Dad says, and smiles at Uncle Ray, who nibbles a drumstick.

Uncle Ray fakes a grin. "Wouldn't miss it for the world."

The phone rings and I answer. "Eckhardt residence."

"This Doc's boy?" a deep masculine voice asks.

"Yes."

"You tell your daddy if he's gonna take care of a nigger whore with AIDS, he's just lost my business."

"Who is this?"

Dial tone.

Dad throws me an inquisitive look.

"Telemarketer," I say as I hang up the receiver. It rings again. "Eckhardt residence."

"This is Gary Mills at the hospital. Let me speak to your father." He sounds angry.

I hand the phone to Dad. "Mr. Mills."

Dad grouses, "What is it, Gary?"

For the next few minutes Dad nods and listens, then says, "No, I will not transfer her. . . . That's not the nurses' or the hospital board's call to make. . . . Gary, I will not give in to their hysteria. And you shouldn't, either. . . . She's my patient and she's going to stay right here until she's healthy enough to leave. Goodbye."

Dad hands me the phone and says, "I've never heard such nonsense in all my life."

I hang up the phone. My dad's battling people who are more paranoid than he is! And he's being so calm, so sensible.

"How's she doing?" Uncle Ray asks Dad.

"Since when do you care?" Mom says to Uncle Ray. "Since when do you care about anyone but yourself?"

We all stare at her in silence.

"That woman's life could very well be ruined because of you!" Mom continues, gathering steam. "And you'll just move on to some other floozy, like you always do. You only hurt people. That's all you've ever done! You swoop in all flashy, and then and then you offer nothing lasting, and—poof!—you're gone."

Mom's bottom lip is quivering as she bolts and disappears down the hallway. Dad gives me a sidelong expression as he stands and goes after her. Uncle Ray and I remain in the silence, and I think about how Mom might still be in love with my uncle Ray. And how she'll never admit it to anyone—including herself.

A half hour later a composed Mom helps me get into my tux and cape while navigating my sling and bandages. Then we all pile into her Buick. As we start down the street, I glance back and see Leo's pickup following us. Uncle Ray sits low in his seat. His hands are trembling.

Cars and people jam the street in front of the junior high school.

"Why, would you look at this turnout," Mom says.

"Uh, Dad, you better drop us off by the front door,"

I say as I look back at Leo's blue truck, four cars behind us. "Uncle Ray can't walk too far."

Dad nods and steers us toward the entrance.

Uncle Ray, Mom, and I join the throngs flowing into the auditorium. I see Leo leap from his truck, but the milling crowd prevents him from catching up to us.

In the foyer Mom stops to greet Principal Cheavers while I lead Uncle Ray down the aisle. I notice an empty seat beside Sheriff Bottoms and his daughter, Geraldine. Before I can tell Uncle Ray to take it, he already has. Leo is standing by the entrance, scanning the crowd.

Backstage is preshow chaos. Kenny Stone, playing the scales on his tuba, sounds like an elephant after a chili-dog–eating contest. Regina, in leg warmers and pink tights, does some sort of stretching exercises. Beside her some guy with a green Mohawk...wait! It's Howard. *I can't believe it's Howard!* He's totally shaved his head except for the spiked green strip down the middle. He's wearing a neon green nylon tracksuit, matching green wristbands, and Adidases.

"Howard?" I say.

"Name's Spike."

"I—I hardly recognized you."

"That's because I'm Spike, the new me I'll be in high school. I'm making my debut tonight."

Is this horrifying or awesome? Both?

"Now excuse me while I prep," he says, and struts away as Charity, looking very sexy in a black and red sequined leotard, white bow tie, and bright red lipstick, rushes up to me.

"Wow! You look great," I say, then pull her into a corner and give her the lowdown about Uncle Ray.

Twenty minutes later the talent show is under way. While the Thornbury triplets, Angie, Alice, and Andrea, play "Three Coins in the Fountain" on their flutes, I peer out from behind the side curtain. Uncle Ray, still seated beside a snoozing Sheriff Bottoms, casts a nervous eye at the door, which Leo and his brother flank like burly sentries.

"Thank you, girls," Principal Cheavers says into the microphone. "Next up we have..." He squints at the paper he's holding. "Spike Bachbaugh!"

Charity and I watch from the wings as the stage goes dark. Moments later a spotlight comes on to reveal Howard posing in the center of the stage, hands in the air, legs spread. A boom box sits behind him. Fast-paced rap music kicks in, and Howard starts break-dancing, spinning and thrusting across the stage like a human funnel cloud. Although he lacks any gymnastic agility or sense of rhythm, Howard's clearly putting everything he has into this high-energy routine. I glance out at the audience: some people look confused, others horrified, many are snickering. Then Howard moonwalks fluidly across the stage—not Michael Jackson, but not bad, either. I can't believe this is Howard, who spends a minimum of four hours a day on the sofa watching TV. With one leg straightened low to the ground, he whips it in circles around his body like a helicopter blade. Who knew?

The spotlight goes out. The music switches to the electrofunk of Styx's "Domo arigato, Mr. Roboto" and a strobe light flashes. Howard, his posture stiff, his joints bent in unnatural positions, keeps pace with the beat and dances like a robot, his angular movements starting and finishing with exaggerated jerks. He has amazing control of his body, a perfect humanoid robot. As the song crescendos, theatrical confusion crosses his face, as if he is malfunctioning. He slowly, mechanically falls to the ground. The song ends with Howard—Spike!—facedown on the stage, his batteries dead.

When the regular stage lights come up, there is silence. I clap loudly and whistle, and suddenly everyone is applauding wildly.

Howard lifts his head, looks out at his newfound fans, and grins.

"Yeah, Spike!" I yell.

From behind the curtain I hear Principal Cheavers say, "Next up we have the Great Linguini and his lovely assistant, Miss Lulu."

Applause. I check to make sure that our phone-booth–like plywood Chinese vanishing box is in place and my top hat is on just right. "Miss Lulu" takes my hand in hers, squeezes it, and smiles reassuringly. God, she's pretty. I inhale deeply as the curtains split and the spotlight blinds us.

With my good arm and Charity's help I perform some standard audience warm-ups: now–you–see–it–now–you–don't card tricks and pulling scarves from the air while telling corny jokes, establishing banter. The applause is generous but not overwhelming—just as I had planned. Then I notice that Sheriff Bottoms is standing up and walking out of the auditorium. Uncle Ray looks at me with pleading eyes.

"And now, for the moment you've all been waiting for," I say quickly. "Our final number, our *pièce de résistance*, our *coup de grâce*. I'm going to make someone from this audience completely disappear right before your very eyes! May I have a volunteer, please? Someone who does not fear the unknown."

About fifty hands shoot up.

"Miss Lulu, will you please select our volunteer."

Charity steps off the stage and into the audience. Placing her hand on her chin, as if having to make a very tough decision, she scans the crowd. Finally she points to Uncle Ray. "I have our volunteer, Great Linguini!"

I glimpse furtively at Leo and his brother, who are halfway down the aisle and exchanging "what the hell is going on?" looks.

Uncle Ray follows Charity onto the stage.

"Sir," I say as I place my right hand on Uncle Ray's shoulder. "Have you ever disappeared before?"

Uncle Ray shakes his head.

"You're a brave soul, a brave soul. Are you prepared to disappear from the world as we know it?"

"Yes, Great Linguini, I am."

"Very well, then."

I pull open the curtain. "Sir, would you please step inside."

The drumroll starts as Uncle Ray gets into the box.

"Good luck in the land of the unknown," I say.

He looks me in the eye and whispers, "Thanks for everything, kid."

A knot rises in my throat. Swallowing hard, I pull the curtain shut and wave my wand. The drumroll swells. Charity spins the box around three times as I watch Leo and his brother creep down the aisle toward the stage.

"Miss Lulu" stops the box, leaving the curtain side facing the audience. The drumroll crescendos. Then, a rapt silence. I pull back the curtain: Uncle Ray is gone. Applause erupts!

I am taking my bow when Leo and his brother barge onstage. They search the empty box: tearing back the curtain, shaking it, looking all around it.

"What'd you do with him?!" Leo asks me while his brother tears the box to splinters.

I smirk. "A magician never gives away his s—"

He reaches out and clutches my neck with his go-rilla hands, choking me. "Where is he?!"

The audience roars with laughter!

"Where is he?!" He shakes me violently.

I can't breathe. I try prying off his grip but it is steel.

"Stop it!" Charity screams, and pounds him with her fists. "Let go of him!"

I am going to be murdered right in front of my parents, my teachers, my friends—while they are laughing, stamping their feet, having a good old time. I have the attention I always craved, and I'm going to die for it.

Their laughter soon mutes and my eyes go dim as consciousness fades. *Everything is so quiet and peaceful in the darkness. I am three years old, lying in bed in my blue feet pajamas, while Mom reads me* Are You My Mother? *I am around five, sitting with Dad as we ride the kiddy train around Harker Park. I am ten, looking down at Grandpa Eckhardt all waxy and sleeping in his casket at church. It is night on a gravel road and Uncle Ray is teaching me to drive his Corvette. I am sitting with Charity and Howard at the Frosty Queen and watching Cookie step off that bus.*

I hear the audience again. But they aren't laughing. They sound stirred up, angry even. When I come to, I am staring up at the stage lights. Charity's gorgeous face is hovering above me. "Les," she says. "Les, it's me."

"Can you hear me, buddy?" Howard asks.

I am lying on the floor of the stage, my neck throbbing.

Nearby, I see Leo doubled over in agony, gripping his hand. "You bit me, you bitch," he yells. "You bit me!"

Dad and Mom soon join Charity's and Howard's hovering faces.

"Les, it's Dad."

"Honey, are you all right?" Mom asks tearfully.

I slowly sit up as Sheriff Bottoms lumbers onto the stage and handcuffs Leo to his brother.

Mom, Dad, Charity, and Howard are pulling me to my feet when I hear the applause. I look out and see all of Harker City Junior High—heck, pretty much my entire hometown—rise to its feet, clapping and cheering. For me.

Life is so . . . odd. But cool!

The moment I can, I slip out the back door of the auditorium. A train engine bellows in the distance, and I move as fast as I can down Walnut Street hill to the rail yard. A freight train is rumbling out of town, gaining steam fast. I come to a stop beside the vibrating tracks, my chest heaving, and eye the passing boxcars. Up ahead I spot a man leaning out of one. Uncle Ray. Waving and smiling big. "Hey, kid! We did it!"

I run alongside his boxcar, calling out over the clanging wheels, "Be careful, Uncle Ray!"

"Don't you worry about me!"

The train is going too fast for me to keep up. As I slow, Uncle Ray turns around and yells, "Onward and upward, kid!"

"I will! Thanks, Uncle Ray!" I yell back.

As he retreats from view, I feel closer to him than

ever. Everything about him, including his flaws, feels larger than life. It's easy to see why everyone falls for him. Then, in a whoosh, the rattling train and my uncle are gone. I watch the diminishing red caboose light reflect off the shiny rails until all is silent and dark.

"They caught the Kansas City killer last night in Louisiana," Dad says into his newspaper the next morning at breakfast. "His name is Sam Hanlan. Know what? He looks a little like Ray. Say, is Ray awake?"

I hand Dad the envelope Uncle Ray asked me to give him.

"What's that?" Mom asks as she comes around the island carrying a plate of toast.

Dad reads the note, says nothing, and hands it to Mom. After finishing it, she's quiet a moment, then says, "He's off into the night, just like he came."

She shakes her head, crosses the kitchen, and places the letter in the trash. "Some people never change."

"He says he's sorry," Dad reminds her. "He thanks us."

Mom slams the plate on the built-ins. "And what good is it?! Tell me, Roger, what good is it?! He got what he wanted from us and he left." Mom takes in a deep breath, then exhales. "Can we please forget he was ever here? Please?"

"Yes, dear."

I'll never forget it. None of us will.

It is a few hours later, when I'm in my room pulling on my sneakers to go visit Cookie at the hospital, that the phone rings.

"Did you hear about Charity?" It's Howard.

"Hear what?" I ask.

"Supposedly, she put the moves on Kristy Lynn last night, and Kristy Lynn's mom and dad found out and want Charity kicked out of school."

I hang up the phone and sprint to Charity's house, where Reverend Bachbaugh's Chrysler is parked in the driveway. Breathless, I peer through the screen door and see Howard's dad sitting on the sofa talking with Charity's grandma. A tall, thin man with dark-brown hair and Charity's blue eyes answers the door.

"I'm here to see Charity," I say, winded.

"She's not up to seeing anyone today."

"Please, sir. I'm her friend Les. I think she'll want to see me."

"She's mentioned you," he says, and opens the door the rest of the way. "Upstairs, first door on the right."

Reverend Bachbaugh and Charity's worried-looking grandmother look up as I breeze past. Upstairs I knock on her closed door, which features a black-and-white picture of a pretty old-time movie actress with Charity's black helmet-like hairdo.

"Charity, it's Les."

"It's open."

Charity is sitting up in bed, her back against the headboard, her knees drawn to her chest. She is in gray sweats; her eyes are red and puffy.

"Hey," I say as I step inside, closing the door behind me.

"Just say it: you were completely right. It was stupid and selfish of me to try anything." She shakes her head. "I mean, what was I thinking? Her parents had a crucifix or a Jesus portrait or a statue on almost every wall and tabletop in the house—there's even one hanging over the toilet!"

I can't help but laugh a little. She glances out the window as I sit on the edge of the bed. Springs creak under my weight.

"Last night, when I kissed her, she seemed really into it—just like that first time." She speaks slowly, her gaze fixed somewhere out the window. "It was beautiful. I felt a real connection with her. We—then, all of a sudden, it was as if a switch had been thrown in her head: she pushed me away, saying she wasn't gay and that we both needed to pray for forgiveness. I tried to tell her everything was all right, that there's nothing wrong with having feelings for someone, but she just got more and more upset, until she was screaming that she wasn't some dirty, perverted dyke. Oh, and she called me 'blasphemous.'

"Then her mom came running in, and Kristy Lynn told her I was trying to turn her into a lesbian. Her mother went ballistic, calling me a whore and a sinner. I thought she was going to hit me. Then her dad showed up and both parents started screaming at me, telling me I was going to hell. It was a nightmare."

"I'm really sorry," I say.

"Her dad called my dad, screaming to 'get her out of our house,' then he informed me he was going to see to it that I was kicked out of school, and out of town if he can manage it."

"What an idiot," I say. "How'd your dad take it?"

"It's weird. He didn't even seem surprised. Like he knew something like this might happen. My grandmother, on the other hand, is a basket case—you'd think I'd taken up Satanism or something. She and that pompous minister of hers have been trying to get me to pray with them all morning." She pauses; then her tone turns somber. "Here's the thing: beneath it all I know Kristy Lynn really likes me—maybe even loves me. She's just terrified of her true feelings. Exactly as Cookie predicted . . ."

Her eyes tear up and her face crumples. Reaching

over, I place my arms around her quaking shoulders. I so want to tell her everything will work out for the best, but I can't honestly say it.

"My life is over," she says, pulling back and wiping her eyes with the back of her hand.

I retrieve a tissue from the nightstand, where a Magic 8–Ball rests beside a lamp. "C'mon," I say. "It's not over."

"I'll always be a fucking freak. You said yourself— I'm unnatural."

"I didn't mean it."

She stares at me through bloodshot eyes. "You tell me, how can my life ever be good?" she asks. "If I'm true to who I am, I'll always be an awful person to most people."

"Since when do you care what most people think?"

"Easy for you to say, you're straight. People don't hate you."

All this pain, all this drama, because she's attracted to girls, just like I am. Amazing. We sit in silence for the longest moment.

"How am I supposed to face everyone at school?" she asks.

"I'll stand up for you."

"You sure you want to put yourself through that? A lot of people will think you're guilty by association. . . ."

"Most people think I'm gay anyway," I say.

"You're so not," she says, and smiles a little. "You're not that good a dresser."

"Thanks a lot."

"And you have no idea what to do with your hair." She leans forward, throws her arms around my neck, and whispers, "But you've been my only real friend here." ·

We hold each other for a while. When she pulls back, I see she is wiping tears again. I guess I do mean something to her.

There's a knock at the door.

"Charity, honey," her grandmother says through the door. "May Pastor Bachbaugh and I talk to you?"

"No!" Charity yells.

After a pause Reverend Bachbaugh's deep pulpit-voice calls out, "Charity, let the Lord heal your soul and show you the way...."

The door is starting to open when Charity grabs the plastic Magic 8–Ball and hurls it, yelling, "Go away!" The door abruptly closes, and we hear shoes scurry down the stairs.

I go over and pick up the 8–Ball. "Says 'Ignore bad advice and listen only to your handsomest friends.'"

She starts to crack up, and then I do, too. We laugh for the longest time—it's like we can't stop, like we have to laugh or else we'll lose our minds. By the time our giggling fit dies out, we're both lying side by side on her bed, with tears streaking down our faces.

Looking around, I see more black-and-white posters of the mesmerizing beauty with the black helmet hair and severe bangs.

"Who is that?"

"That's Louise Brooks, my idol," she says.

"Ah, the movie actress you told me about," I say. "Why is she your idol?"

She reaches under the bed, hands me a thick photo album, and shows me the vast collection of Louise Brooks memorabilia she's picked up at flea markets and garage sales over the years.

"Lulu was a free spirit," Charity says, "intellectually, artistically, sexually. And, believe it or not, she was from Kansas!"

"Cool. What happened to her?"

"At the height of her fame she demanded to be paid what men were making in the movies—and the studios blacklisted her."

She hands me a copy of a book entitled *Lulu in Hollywood*. "It's all in her autobiography, which is completely fascinating."

I open to the part of the book with the pictures.

"Lulu once said, 'I have a gift for enraging people. But if I ever bore you, it will be with a knife.' I love that."

"Yeah, that's great."

"She was way ahead of her time," she says, and points to a photo of a very young Louise wearing a dance costume with a wide skirt. "Y'know, she started out as a dancer in Wichita."

"Wonder if Cookie's ever heard of her?" I ask.

"Hey, how's Cookie doing?!"

"Oh my God, Cookie!" I jump up. "I have to go see her at the hospital."

"Let's go."

Might as well gather all the town misfits in one place.

When we arrive at the hospital, the ISOLATION sign is no longer hanging on Cookie's door. Her bed has been stripped, and the noxious stench of bleach accosts my nose. A rotund nurse in mask and gloves is scrubbing everything with a large brush.

"Where is she?" I ask.

The woman stops scrubbing and looks at me, puzzled.

"The woman who was staying here," I blurt out frantically. "Cookie. Where is she?!"

"Discharged," she drawls. "Left a couple hours ago."

My heart is pounding. "Where'd she go?"

"To catch the four o'clock bus."

The clock on the wall reads 3:50. I run into the hall–

way and spot Dad sitting at the nurses' desk, writing in a chart.

"Dad, I need you to drive us somewhere right now."

He looks at me over his reading glasses.

"It's important." I tug on his arm.

"Les, I have patients waiting—"

"She's leaving town in ten minutes. Please, Dad!"

Dad, Charity, and I are silent on the car ride to the Frosty Queen. As we turn into the lot, I see Cookie sitting on the bus-stop bench, her zebra-print suitcase beside her, Mr. Mister on her lap.

"You don't have to wait," I say to Dad as I fling open the door and dash out.

Mr. Mister yips at the sight of us, shoots off her lap, and waggles over to me.

I scoop him up and scratch under his chin.

Cookie makes a visor with her hands, then jumps to her feet. "Les! Charity!"

"Would have been here sooner if I'd known," I say as I set Mr. Mister down.

"I'm so glad you made it," she says.

"You're okay?" Charity asks.

"I gotta take the antibiotics for a little while longer," Cookie says. "But looks like the baby and me are gonna be A-OK, thanks to your folks. You know, Ray called me last night. Said he was leaving town. That he was sorry about everything but that he couldn't see this through. He wished me luck. I was surprised he called at all. It was more than I expected."

I lower my voice so that Dad, who is leaning against his car and smoking a pipe, can't hear. "But are you going to be okay? I mean, how're you going to survive?"

She smiles. "In case you haven't noticed, this Cookie, she don't crumble."

Charity laughs.

"But what about wanting a father for your child?"

"Bein' in the hospital got me to thinkin' that the baby's health is the most important thing. I have a strong sense everything's gonna work out just fine for me and the kid."

I hear the rumble of the bus behind me and I suddenly feel nervous.

"Before I go, Les, there's something you should know," Cookie says. "I did a psychic reading on you the first time I met you. Wanna know what I saw?"

"Is it bad?" I ask.

"The next four years will be difficult for you," Cookie says. "You won't fit in, you'll be very lonely at times. But you need to be patient, you need to stay yourself, because things will change and you will get out of this town. You're gonna go far in life, Les."

"But will I ever find . . . you know?" I ask.

"Not till later, but you will eventually make a very special woman very happy."

"Hot damn!" I yell, and Charity high-fives me.

Cookie places her hand beside her mouth and whispers, "Don't tell your dad this, but you'll never be no doctor."

The bus pulls in and hisses to a stop.

"Will I be?" Charity asks.

"Yes," Cookie says. "I have a sense that you will be a healer."

I high-five Charity back.

"If I have a boy, I'm naming him Roger."

The horse-faced bus driver steps down and asks us, "Three for Kansas City?"

"Just one," Cookie says.

"That your suitcase, ma'am?"

She nods. He takes it and stashes it in the baggage compartment.

Cookie picks up Mr. Mister and smiles at me. "Guess this is it, huh?"

I blink hard and nod.

"Can I visit you and the baby sometime?" I ask.

She turns and smiles. "Of course. I'd like that very much." She waves at Dad and blows him a kiss.

"Good luck," Charity says, gives Cookie a squeeze, then goes and stands with Dad.

I run up and hug Cookie. Mmm, she feels great.

"I'll write," she says.

"And I'll write you back."

I get a peck on the cheek before she climbs aboard. She holds Mr. Mister up to the window, raises his little paw, and makes a waving gesture at us. The bus engine groans to life, exhaust belches up, and they roll away. Soon they are lumbering onto the highway, heading north, becoming smaller and smaller in the wavelets of heat.

I keep my back to Dad and Charity, not wanting to let them see me cry. After a few moments I swipe my eyes quickly.

"You know, the whole town's talking about what your friend Charity tried to do to Kristy Lynn," Mom says at the breakfast table as she forks into her scrambled eggs.

I say nothing as I chew my burnt bacon.

Mom clears her throat. "Did you know Charity was... that way?"

On my right I see Dad peek a curious eye over the Wichita newspaper.

"Yeah, I knew."

"Why, for heaven's sake, didn't you say something?" Mom asks.

"Why would I?"

"I don't know," Mom says. "Maybe we could've helped her in some way."

I look at Mom a long moment and say, "I guess we all have secrets we just have to keep."

Mom stares back at me, and something tells me she knows I know about her big secret.

"Charity didn't do anything Kristy Lynn didn't invite," I say.

Mom's mouth falls open a little.

Dad ruffles his newspaper in that way he does that announces: "All right, enough with this topic." As he turns the page, I see a small headline in the arts section: "Screen Legend Louise Brooks Retrospective Tonight!"

I watch as Charity, seated on the edge of her bed, shakes her head in disbelief at the Louise Brooks article. "This is a dream come true."

I'm so happy to give her something to get her mind off the train wreck that is her life.

"We have to go!" She leaps up and hugs me. "We have to! This is so great!"

"Can your dad take us?" I ask.

She shakes her head. "He won't get back from work till Tuesday night. And my grandma doesn't drive. Can you ask your parents?"

"I can, but don't get your hopes up."

She takes my hand and squeezes it. "Les, we *have* to go to this."

***

"I don't think so," Mom says as she knits an afghan on the sofa.

"Why not?" I ask. I'm standing in front of the TV, which features a PBS documentary about puffins. Dad, from his recliner, strains to see around me.

"Tomorrow's Memorial Day," I say. "You and Dad don't have to work."

"Who is this—Louise Brooks, did you say her name was?"

"She's a—a cinematic legend. And Charity's idol. There's, you know, real historical value to us attending this."

"I think Charity has more than enough to deal with right now, don't you?"

Dad pipes up with: "Everyone knows Wichita isn't safe at night. . . ."

"And gas prices are through the roof," Mom choruses.

"We never go anywhere, we never do anything!" flies out of my mouth.

Mom and Dad look at me, wide-eyed.

"You're too young to realize this now," Dad says, "but your welfare has always been our first concern."

Mom nods.

"Jesus Christ!" I yell. "Don't use me as an excuse for your fear of living. You do that *all the time*."

Mom gasps. "You know better than to take the Lord's name in vain in this house, young man!"

"They're just words," I say. "They don't kill people. They're just words. God won't strike me dead."

Mom whirls to Dad. "It's that brother of yours. Didn't I tell you he would influence our Lester negatively!"

"*You're* influencing me negatively!" I yell. "You're smothering me. I have nothing in this place!"

"Roger, are you going to let him get away with saying these awful things?"

"Let him speak, Mother."

"Don't you see you're *both* driving me away from you?" I say. "Unless you want me to turn out like Uncle Ray and run away for good like he did, you have to ease up, you have to stop being so scared of everything. We have to go somewhere...do something... and stop living like we do every damn day!"

Mom and Dad stare at me in unblinking silence.

"Things can't stay the way they are," I say. "Not anymore. Not ever again."

That evening Mom and Dad drive Charity and me to Wichita. Mom and Dad act as if nothing has happened to Charity. (I feared they'd be overly nice, but they treat her like they'd treat Howard or anyone else.) Charity and Dad talk a lot about the courses she needs to take in high school to prepare for becoming a doctor.

The Louise Brooks tribute is held in the Orphcum, a downtown movie palace. It's the biggest theater I've been in, and it's so packed we have to sit in the rear balcony. Dad mumbles something to Mom about how the old balcony might collapse under all the weight. Mom pats his hand reassuringly. A dark-haired man in horn-rimmed glasses and a brown bow tie takes the stage, introducing himself as Dr. Frank Baker, a film historian at Wichita State University.

With a slight lisp, he says into the microphone, "The film critic Ado Kyrou once said, 'Louise Brooks is the only woman who had the ability to transfigure no matter what film into a masterpiece.... Louise is the perfect apparition, the dream woman, the being without whom the cinema would be a poor thing.'"

I don't hear much of what else he says. I'm too taken in by the ornate molding on the ceiling, the big crystal chandeliers, all the people.

Charity whispers to me, "This is the same theater Louise danced ballet in as a girl."

Soon the lights dim and organ music starts. A black-and-white title flickers on-screen: *Pandora's Box.* I'm fully expecting to be bored by a silent movie made in 1929. Within minutes I'm hooked.

A very sexy Louise Brooks, called Lulu in the movie, isn't a hammy old-time actress at all. With her trademark black hair and severe bangs, she plays a dance-hall girl with a dazzling smile and naughty moves. In the fast-paced story she breaks up her boyfriend's impending marriage to another woman, then winds up hiding out with her lover's grown son, who is a sleazy gambler. There's lust, gambling, adults cheating on each other, hookers, murders, and even lesbians (Lulu dances with a woman she's attracted to on her wedding day!). No wonder Charity idolizes her. And at the breath-stealing end Lulu takes a final lover, who turns out to be none other than Jack the Ripper himself, and he murders her!

When "The End" flashes on-screen, everyone

applauds like crazy. The lights come up, and an old woman in a wheelchair is rolled out onstage by a tall bald man in a suit. Charity is the first on her feet, and by far the loudest clapper. I can't see much of Miss Brooks from where we're sitting, just that her long hair is a dark gray and she looks to have an oxygen tank beside her chair.

The bald man turns out to be the mayor of Wichita. He's about to give Louise the key to the city when Charity bolts into the aisle and toward the exit as if the building is on fire. Where is she going? I run after her.

"What's up?" I call out as I chase her down the stairway.

"I have to meet her!"

"Just don't . . ."

In the downstairs part of the theater I stand with Charity along the back wall while the mayor babbles about what an honor it is to have Miss Brooks back in Wichita. I can see Louise better from here, but still not great. A small plastic tube is hooked under her nose. Her face is remarkably wrinkle free, and her eyes are still stunners.

"She's so beautiful," Charity whispers. I've never seen Charity so excited about anything (except for maybe Kristy Lynn).

The mayor hands the microphone to Louise. In a forceful but winded voice she says, "Thank you. I feel that today I have finally made peace with my home-town. Or perhaps it's made peace with me."

Pictures are taken, more applause.

"Miss Brooks will now be greeting some people on the stage," the mayor announces. No sooner does he say this than Charity scrambles down the aisle, where a line is fast forming. I struggle to keep up with her. We wait in line for twenty minutes as fans slowly file past the star, shaking her hand and getting her autograph. Charity's eyes don't deviate from Louise for a second. It's when Louise starts to cough heavily that the mayor says over the microphone, "I'm sorry but Miss Brooks won't be seeing anyone else...."

Charity jumps the line—jumps the line!—and bounds up onto the stage. I start to go after her but a security guard lays his big mitts on me.

Charity kneels before Miss Brooks, who smiles. They talk for a good minute—it looks like a fairly intense conversation, with Charity nodding a lot. Finally Miss Brooks is wheeled offstage and Charity lopes back my way. She doesn't look elated, which surprises me. She looks, well, a little let down.

Later Charity and I amble along the path by the Arkansas River, the sun-reflected skyline of downtown Wichita towering behind us. Charity has been pretty subdued and preoccupied since meeting her idol.

"Y'mind telling me what you and Louise talked about?" I ask.

"She told me she was flattered she's my idol,"

Charity says, "but that I really don't know her. And that if I did know her, I wouldn't idolize her."

"Strange thing to tell a fan."

"Then she said, 'Imitation is suicide.' "

"Wow."

" 'But I respect everything you stand for, everything you've done,' I told her. Her response was: 'It's more important you find out who you are and what you're capable of.'"

I glance back at Mom and Dad strolling about fifty feet behind us. Dad's arm is around Mom and he kisses her cheek—something he would *never* dare do in downtown Harker City.

Charity stops and leans against the wooden railing. "Problem is, Les, I'm not exactly sure who I am."

"Think I know what you mean."

"Do you? Sometimes I feel like there's nothing to me. That's what I love so much about Louise. She's always had courage, she always knew what she wanted, never cared what others thought. Or so I thought."

Looking out over the brownish rippling water, I say, "You know, I idolized my uncle Ray. He was always so smooth, so cool. I wanted to be him. And then he came to stay with us . . . and, well, I realized I don't want to be him. Still, I really admire the guy."

She turns to me and says, "You know something, I think Kristy Lynn did me a huge favor. Thanks to her, I can't pretend any longer. Till now no one at school, besides you, knew the real me. Now everyone does.

Like it or not, I have to be me when I go back and face everyone on Tuesday. The problem is, it scares me half to death."

I can't help but laugh. "It's kinda like me. I have to figure out how not to impersonate Uncle Ray, and still talk to girls."

"Well, Booger, looks like we've got our work cut out for us."